Love Stor
Of
Shimla Hills

Love Stories Of Shimla Hills

Minakshi Chaudhry

Rupa・Co

Copyright © Minakshi Chaudhry 2010

First Published 2010
Second Impression 2011

Published by
Rupa Publications India Pvt. Ltd.
7/16, Ansari Road, Daryaganj,
New Delhi 110 002

Sales Centres:
Allahabad Bengaluru Chennai
Hyderabad Jaipur Kathmandu
Kolkata Mumbai

All rights reserved.
No part of this publication may be reproduced, stored in a
retrieval system, or transmitted, in any form or by any means,
electronic, mechanical, photocopying, recording or otherwise,
without the prior permission of the publishers.

The author asserts the moral right to be identified
as the author of this work

Typeset by
Mindways Design
1410 Chiranjiv Tower
43 Nehru Place
New Delhi 110 019

Printed in India by
Nutech Photolithographers
B-240, Okhla Industrial Area, Phase-I,
New Delhi 110 020, India

To My Husband
Rakesh

*The word love can be explained in thousands of ways,
But the only word that comes to my mind is you.*

Anon

Contents

Acknowledgements *ix*
Preface *xi*
Author's Note *xix*

1 Love Story of A *Sati* — *1*
2 The Surprise — 11
3 When Rani Became A Boy — 16
4 Scandal Point — 22
5 The Princess — 29
6 Amrita Sher-Gil — 38
7 A Spiritual Bond: Edwina And Jawahar Lal Nehru — 49
8 My Marriages . . . The *Reet* — 60
9 Love In Simla — 71
10 A Love Song That Changed Their Lives — 77
11 Forever Twenty — 84
12 Everlasting Love — 95

13 The Sanyasi	104
14 The Ghost Who Loved	114
15 Love@www	125
16 My Parents' Love Story	134

| *Glossary* | 143 |
| *References* | 147 |

Acknowledgements

I am thankful to my family for their love and patience, affection and understanding – parents-in-laws, parents, Anu didi, Dalbir, Deepika, Chandni, Seema didi, Neeraj, Deepak, Pooja and Shalini. Without Rakesh, my soulmate, this book would not have been possible.

Constructive criticism of so many friends helped in this endeavour – Gopal, Lalit, Shashikant, Dr Hardayal, Anand Noatay, Akshiti, Dr R.K. Gupta, Deepshikha, Shalu, Kalpana, Richa, Loveleen, Manu, Hemlata, Ashwani, Sapna, Ashok, Shakti, Shaily, Saloni, Kamal, Sneh, Poonam, Usha, Jaideep Negi, Joginder Kanwar, Chaman Singh bhaiya, Pathick, Shekhar, Jyoti, Anilkant.

I also thank Ramesh and Lakshmi for their support at home.

I sincerely thank my teacher Prof Vepa Rao in supporting and guiding me in all my writing projects. Special thanks are due to the editorial team at Rupa especially Sumana who went through the manuscript meticulously, edited and tightened the stories. Special thanks to Mr R.K. Mehra of Rupa for his encouragement and support.

Preface

The fragrance of carefree, joyous wild flowers; the pearl-like rain drops; the floating snow; the thick forest of deodar, oak and rhododendron – whispering and exchanging tales with the passing, cool scented breeze; the cascading bluish green hills; the setting sun throwing myriad hues of red on the horizon – what better place to be in love than Shimla hills.

So many people shared their extraordinary love tales with me as we sat watching the flaming evening colours spread across horizon on rain-washed evenings, on fog-filled monsoon days, on bright summer days when sky was the bluest and on winter days when the hills were covered in white. And I thought Shimla is an ideal place to set every heart on fire. I realised that these tales are inseparable from the ambiance of Shimla Hills.

As I worked on these tales – talking to innumerable people, researching, going through old records, I found that everyone – rich-poor, male-female, celebrity-common man had a love story which was precious to each one of them. 'Their' story was the best and their love was the purest, the most true, the most unique. As some of my narrators checked the stories and went through them, I was surprised, not only by their involvement in the story but their persistence for it to be very, very real without a single word or phrase changed.

Writing this book was special for me, nothing can be more serious than love, the emotion without which the world is lifeless, which everyone needs and craves for.

I myself have loved and been loved truly and that is the joy of my life. I dread to even think what my life would have been if my 'love' was not with me. It is this love that makes me go on despite all odds. Like me there must be so many others who have gone through this beautiful relationship and reached the pinnacle where everything – ambition, materialism, success, achievement, fame and glory fades.

Moreover, I wanted to explore the theme of love, love in the sense of not only the physical kind, but deeper, more intense, the very essence of life. I was not interested in the scandalous angle but in the general feel-good factor. The purpose is to make these stories immortal and to celebrate love; not to defame, malign or hurt anyone's feelings.

It was a difficult task in the sense that though every human being has a love story but few want to share it. The reason may be one or manifold – shyness, hesitation, what will people say, circumstances, a desire to keep it to oneself, too personal and so on. Many were in Catch 22 situation to tell or not to tell.

It brought back memories of a decade back when I had wandered around the hills investigating and collecting Ghost

PREFACE | xiii

Stories and was subjected to ridicule – *bhoot! Aaj ki duniya mein, kahan se aaye ho?* (Ghosts! In today's' world, where have you come from?) I would be interviewed by one and all; I was informally detained by the army suspecting me to be a spy; attacked by a priest who thought I must be a *churail* incarnate; took shelter in Shimla jail when I was being charged by two *lathi* wielding men; chased by pack of dogs unleashed by a man who owned a garden which was rumoured to be haunted. This time it was less harrowing but equally exasperating experience. There was less of ridicule and jest but people were more interested in knowing other people's love stories than willing to share their own.

The shy smile of an octogenarian; the giggles and blushes of a housewife; the bright spark lighting the eyes of a *golgappa* vendor; the surprised look on the face of young children as their mother narrated her love story; the nostalgic memory of a wife for a husband who was with her for more than fifty years. On the other hand the adamancy of a couple who had eloped but were not ready to admit that they loved each other; the callousness of a youngster – what love, no time for romance, careers have to be built; it is too personal what will my wife say; I do not want it to be in the book; ours was not a love story; I can tell you so many scandalous tales if you want but no love story . . . and so on . . . Every day was a new experience for me!

I met so many people who were open and ready to share their love tale with me and realised they were far more happy and satisfied whether their stories had the ending they would have liked or not.

I also felt sad when I talked to those who concluded that I was after scandalous, illicit and secretive love affairs, something for the gossip mongers to chew on, to malign and defame. I was disheartened when many reacted defensively – why was I asking them; what do they know about love; they don't have a love story; why should they – they are good people.

For others it took a lot of time to understand that love is strength, sacrifice, forgiveness, joy, happiness and the very thing which brings light in the lives of everyone. I am thankful to all those who understood this and supported me wholeheartedly.

I collected more than fifty stories and chose sixteen in this volume highlighting people's relationship in Shimla hills through time. The collection also shows how the theme of love changed in different decades starting from nineteen fifties. It seems every decade had its own unique trend of wooing and expressing love, but that thrill, that sensation, that glow on face and that twinkle in the eye . . . remains the same.

Young lovers today have SMS, phone calls and the net to connect with each other but long back in fifties and sixties it were rose-scented handwritten notes and Urdu couplets that were exchanged through messengers secretly . . . girls kept these notes neatly folded under the pillow in the night or in the books with rose petals and re-read each word hundred times a day.

PREFACE | xv

Couplet by Meer written on a handmade paper – *nazuki uske lab ki kya kahiye, pankhuri ek gulab ki si hai/'meer' un neembaaz ankhon mein, saari masti sharab ki si hai* – was enough to make a girl blissfully happy. In seventies love was secretive and it was social disgrace if it came out in the open. To convince families was a Herculean task and so many strategies were thought of. With eighties started the struggle against the barriers of caste and region ... and another trend began when Maruti Omni started the taxi-boom in the Shimla Hills. So many girls eloped with taxi drivers! And then marriage by running away became a trend of sorts which made parents of young boys and girls fret and fear. Some temples became popular as marriage temples where you could get married in minutes before your parents found out or caught up with you. This tide went on till early nineties and then ebbed slowly. Love came out of closet and young lovers shed many inhibitions just as the lovers of sixties and seventies became parents. Love bloomed and now it is no longer a stigma. Obstacles and problems are still there, but this has always been so and will always be so.

Moreover, the magic of romance here goes back to centuries. Love legends and ballads echoed in Shimla hills even when Simla was Shyamla or Shumlah and was no more than a 'middling size village where a fakir gave water to travelers.' These tales are sung in local fairs and festivals even now.

Life in hills took a gay turn when Lord Amherst started the summer move in 1827. Fun, frolic, romance, secret rendezvous, mischievous pranks, flirtations, intrigues and jealousies became integral part of the social life in Simla.

Simla came to be known as 'the heavenly melting pot for socially aspiring, flirtatious women'. Young girls flocked the town in search of husbands and competed with 'flirty army and Civil Service wives and grass widows'.

Rudyard Kipling in his *Plain Tales from the Hills* depicted and caricatured the life in Simla by hinting about flirtatious life, romantic flings and loose living:

> *Amen! Here ends the comedy*
> *Where it began in all good will,*
> *Since Love and leave together flee*
> *As driven mist on Jakko Hill!*

Towards the end of nineteenth century Peliti's was the fashionable hotel in Simla. . . . It was at Peliti's that Mrs Hauksbee had tiffin with Mr Bremmil while Mrs Bremmil remained at home and wept into an empty cradle. Kipling satirised this life in his lines put in the mouth of a virtuous monkey (*Bandar*) who boasted:

> *Never in my life*
> *Have I flirted at Peliti's with another Bandar's wife.*

For maharajas, rajas and other rich and affluent Indians Simla became their favourite summer sojourn. The Maharajah of Patiala would move to his Simla palace for six months of partying, tennis, cricket and royal hunting with his retinue of 1,000 including wives, mistresses, secretariat and stables.

Even though Simla lost some of its importance and much of its population immediately after Independence yet it retained the glamour and reputation of being an elite station. And love continued to bloom....

Presently, Shimla is the ideal destination for honeymooners and there are innumerable love tales waiting to be discovered and shared.

Minakshi Chaudhry

Author's Note

These stories depict love and romance in the Shimla Hills from the seventeenth century to the twenty-first century. They not only document love shared by ordinary people and celebrities through the centuries but also portray the life, customs, culture, changing socio-cultural mosaic, places, environment and ambience of Shimla.

These are true stories. Names and situations have been changed in some cases on request in order to protect identity. In other cases names, places and situations are as narrated.

The historical romances included in the book are also true. These are supported by references wherever required. I have deliberately not fictionalised the narrative in these cases to retain the original flavour and to maintain the authenticity of these tales.

SIMLA changed officially to SHIMLA in the beginning of the 1980s but I have retained both spellings as used by the narrators and also depending upon the context.

1

Love Story of A *Satī*

'So, you are collecting love stories,' Mr Meena Ram Sanghaik said.

'Well, yes. You know, real ones with some drama in them,' I replied.

'Drama . . . hum . . . I can tell you a story which has a lot of drama in it.'

'Oh.' I am inquisitive but a little in doubt as to what kind of story this elderly man knows.

'There is passion, there is bravery, there is sacrifice, there is freedom and there is death,' he says softly.

I am all ears now.

'Should I sing for you, *beta*?'

Sing? I am skeptical. 'Is it a real story?'

'It is real, as real as any love story can be. And it is old, maybe, 400 years old. It has been passed down the generations orally. I can sing this saga of love and longing for six hours non-stop,' he says with pride.

'Wow, this is a seventeenth-century love tale.' I get excited. 'Is it so long?' I ask him.

'Yes, it is long. The song captures every detail in the lives of the main characters.'

It must be some epic, I wonder. Before I can ask any other question, the old man starts to sing . . . eyes closed, his wrinkled face lit up and I can see that he is fully involved in the emotions of Boiya, Lala, Ghaintu . . . the main characters . . . .

I too am transported 400 years back to a different world . . . .

ೞ

Every one knows the names of brave Lala and Boiya . . . the brothers who hail from Thundal in the upper Simla hills. Tales of their valour are sung by many.

They have attained the status of folk heroes at a young age. None can match them. Their fame and prominence has spread far and wide, not only as brave men but also as the great Thoda players. None dares to contest the duo. Whoever foolish enough to do so has been slain by the two. They are not only brothers but close friends. In fact, people never take the name of one alone. They are always referred to as Lala–Boiya. Other players dread their presence as they always win.

On one fateful day, the brothers go to Khoda in Balsam State to participate in a Thoda competition. As they near the place they meet several men and women dressed in colourful clothes on their way to the fair and to watch the great Thoda spectacle. Many are humming popular folk-songs to the music of trumpets and drums.

Just short of the playing field, Boiya sees a beautiful lady dressed in a flaming red *kameez* and *suthnu*. She has a multi-hued *chadru* wrapped around her and carries a *hukkah* in her slender hand. Bewitched by her beauty, Boiya asks his brother to enquire who she is . . . .

She is beautiful beyond words, her yellow *dhatu* with an enchanting flower on one side, her delicate neck adorned with a bright necklace, her long dangling ear rings touching her cheeks as she walks . . . the ornaments she is wearing enhance her beauty manifold and Boiya's heart is lost forever.

Lala understands the agony of his love-stricken brother and inquires about her. He tells Boiya, 'The beauty who has stolen your heart, O, my brave brother, is Ghainthu, the daughter of Pammu of Sujra village and daughter-in-law of Mushoo of Bathocha village.'

The brothers reach the arena, the competition is yet to start and players are making their preparations. Boiya's eyes search for Ghainthu in the crowd and soon he locates his love sitting in the ladies' enclosure. The crowd is warming up to a fierce battle between the players. Many have just come to see Lala–Boiya. Suddenly, Boiya starts limping, he says that a thorn has pierced his foot and he needs a needle to take it out. Some players of rival teams heave a sigh of relief for they think that now they stand a chance against the formidable duo but Lala smiles, he knows that Boiya just wants to be near Ghainthu.

Limping, Boiya goes to the ladies section of the crowd and stands near Ghainthu and pretends to take out the thorn with the help of a needle that one of the ladies has given him. He is looking sideways towards the beautiful damsel. Their eyes meet and it is instant love for Gainthu, too. The fair damsel falls for the handsome young man. She is so attracted to the handsome Boiya that her hands start trembling and the *hukkah* that she is carrying slips and falls down. A look can do so much to a loving heart.

As for Boiya, when his eyes meet Ghainthu he feels as if life has gone out of his body for a moment. He loses control over his mind and becomes oblivious of his surroundings.

The battle cries of rival teams bring him back to his senses and, stealing another glance at the most beautiful lady he has ever seen, he rushes towards the playing arena. Ghainthu reciprocates with a smile and his heart starts to dance, he is elated. Never before has Boiya felt so powerful, so fresh before a Thoda competition.

Musicians start playing the tunes to which the players dance and play. Lala–Boiya are so good that people used to say '*yeh chalte hue teer par nishana laga sakte hain*' (they can aim at a moving arrow). The brothers start to win every game and as is the custom, after every win they sing to the chagrin of the losing team, 'we are brave men while you are nothing, not even the dust.'

As expected, the brothers win the championship. They are not only master players but also masters of dance and song so they break into a soulful song and rhythmic dance to celebrate their victory.

Ghainthu cannot stop herself and she joins them in the merriment and starts dancing alongside them. As she dances and sways to the musical beats in the beautiful surroundings her *chadaru* touches Boiya's body and he loses himself completely in her love. She dances so beautifully that Boiya showers silver coins on her.

During this public display of love and affection, Ajooa, the husband of Ghainthu is also present. He turns red with anger as he looks at the open exhibition of emotion by his beautiful wife for another man. He cannot stop himself and he jumps into the arena, abuses Ghainthu and hits her. She feels insulted, leaves the *mela* in a fit of anger.

At home, a tearful Ghainthu tells her father-in-law that she wants to go back to her parents' house. She seeks his permission. The wise father-in-law suspects that something is wrong and tries to judge what exactly happened at the fair which made his *bahu* so upset. He wants to give her time to cool down. So, he asks questions: O, *bahu*, tell me, what did you find the most attractive in the mela, who all were there, were there any good players of Thoda, who dominated the game, who won, who were the good looking and handsome men there, who danced the best?

The *bahu* also understands the intentions of the old man so at first she tells him that his son was the most beautiful and handsome man there. But she cannot keep away her real feelings for long and says that the brave pair of Lala–Boiya was there and they were the bravest men in the mela. They played so well that the elders said that they had not seen such a good game of Thoda in years. She gives away her heart's secret and showers praises on the brothers.

The father-in-law listens with patience and comprehends what has happened. To distract his *bahu's* attention he tells her that she cannot go to her *maika* as some of the players and other guests from the adjoining villages might come to stay the night. The villagers have distributed the guests to every house. The guests will need food and must be looked after. What will they say if they are not attended to in our house which is the best in this village, he asks her.

Ghainthu agrees to cook. The father-in-law now changes his tactics and tells her that he owns a lot of property which, after him, will belong to his son. She listens quietly. To impress her further he tells her to go to the *Chandhar*, the attic of the house and bring some *mash ki daal* to cook for the guests. This is just a ploy. The attic contains jewelry, silver coins and all other valuables of the house. He is sure that when she sees such wealth she will change her mind.

When she returns from the attic the father-in-law asks Ghainthu if she found the *daal*. She says there is no *daal* there. He asks her what she had found then. 'There is some useless stuff there; it stinks, there is *ghaas-phoos* and it is full of animal excreta,' she says. Meanwhile, Boiya has traced her house and arranged to be there as a guest for the night, so both brothers walk towards the house in a boisterous mood. The father-in-law sees the brothers coming and realises that these must be the famous Lala–Boiya whom Ghainthu has praised and fallen for. In anger he unleashes his big, ferocious dog on them and hides himself on the other side of the house. The dog charges menacingly towards the brothers but the two brave brothers catch hold of the dog and kill it in such a manner that when they throw the dog on the floor its spine gets broken into a hundred pieces.

Then, they enter the kitchen where Ghainthu is making *patande*. Boiya, to impress his beloved, starts telling her about his village: here in this village you eat *patande* with only one vegetable whereas in my lovely Thundal there are several vegetables to be had; here in this village you cook only one cereal but in my prosperous Thundal you get seven kinds of cereals; here you have a small house, but in my Thundal I not only have a huge house but I also have four *dogris*; these *dogris*, the summer homes, are spread from hill-top to the valley floor; so vast is my land that while in one *dogri* barley is getting ripened, wheat is getting ready for harvest in the other; here you work both inside and outside the house whereas in my Thundal ladies work only inside the house; all heavy work is done by the labourers whom we have in plenty; here you do all the work but in my Thundal there will be so many servants that you will call for one but many will come running; as compared to your small hamlet my village is so big that I have sixty cousins who are handsome like me; my village is so large that there is a queue of sixty ladies near the well.

Ghainthu is so impressed that in the dead of night she leaves her in-laws' house with Lala–Boiya and heads for her dream land – Thundal.

There they live happily and Ghainthu feels secure in the love of Boiya. When everything is going smoothly life takes another turn.

While the brothers have gone to play Thoda in an adjoining village, eighteen *sevaks* of the Raja of Jubbal visit their village. These *sevaks* have heard about the beauty of Ghainthu and know that she has left her husband for the brave Boiya. They are aware of the absence of Boiya so they start teasing and taunting her. They speak against Boiya and advise her to come with them.

Ghainthu is disturbed. Helplessly she walks up and down the house praying for the early return of her husband and his brother. She looks anxiously towards the *dhar* (ridge) from where they will appear. Finally, the brothers reach home and she tells them about the insult by the sevaks. She tells them that they taunted not only her but insulted both of them. She starts to cry.

Lala–Boiya become so enraged that the mountains start trembling, birds sense the coming danger and fly away. Animals start making ominous sounds but the *sevaks*, intoxicated with power, fail to notice the alarm bells. The brothers are very angry but they plan their cold-blooded strategy with precision.

They tell Ghainthu to make *siddus* for the guests. Then, the brothers offer them food, pretending they know nothing. Lala asks the *sevaks* to wash their hands first. He takes them to a corner room at the other end of a long corridor away from the kitchen. While Lala sends each one to wash his hands inside the room, Boiya hides behind the door with a sharp weapon. One by one, he kills all the eighteen *sevaks*.

The news spreads through the village and the villagers are frightened. They fear that the Raja of Jubbal will wreck havoc on them for killing his *sevaks*. They plead to the brothers that though everyone loves them dearly and they are the pride of the village, they should leave the village for some time for their own safety and to spare the lives of the innocent villagers. They request them to return after the matter cools down.

So, Lala–Boiya and Ghainthu, accompanied by their cattle, leave Jubbal and go to settle at Kuthar village in the adjoining Balsan State. They also take a *bail* (bull) of the local *devta* of Thundal village as a token of respect and remembrance.

They settle at the new place. However, they miss their village and are often depressed by their self-imposed exile. They long to go back. But then the hands of fate move again and Boiya suddenly dies.

Ghainthu takes the ultimate decision for her love. She feels that everything is lost. He was a man who suffered the agony of losing his land and home for her. She wants to pay back her beloved. She decides to commit *sati* with her husband.

Lala–Boiya belonged to the Rajput clans that had settled in Shimla hills after they fled from Rajasthan when the Mughals were on ascendancy. These families gave full freedom to their women as was the practice before the Mughals. They chose their own husbands, accompanied them in hunting and war. These warrior clans set up small principalities and hill states and brought their customs with them. One such practice was *Sati* where some women voluntarily died at their husband's pyre.

When the Rana of Kuthar gets to know of Ghainthu's plan he tells her that the sati should take place at Kuthar, where Boiya had died. He wants such an auspicious rite to be performed in his village. However, Ghainthu tells him that they did not belong there. Thundal is their homeland. She thanks him for the asylum but tells him that one day they were bound to return to their lovely village Thundal. Now it is her duty to take his body back to his homeland.

The Rana of Kuthar and several others accompany her and witness her act of love and devotion. The place where Ghainthu committed *sati* is still considered sacred.

ೞ

Mesmerised, I heard the last lines of the ballad of Ghainthu and Boiya and watched tears pour down the intense gentle face of the elderly man as he concluded the love epic.

17th century

2

The Surprise

Emily Metcalfe was born in India in 1831. The fate of most of the children of English couples in India who were born at that time was the same. They had to spend their childhood in England thousands of miles away from their parents with their relatives or even with strangers. So, Emily was not six when her mother kissed her goodbye at the deck of a sailing ship in Calcutta.

The brave English ladies who undertook the long and treacherous journey to India in the early eighteenth century were lucky if they arrived safe. The travails of these wives of British officers did not end there; they had to live in a hostile environment in an inhospitable climate. But above everything else they had to live separated from their children. Indeed, they paid a heavier price for serving the Raj than anyone realises now. During the period of British rule in India hundreds of British children who were born here grew up barely knowing their parents and year after year weeping mothers took their children down to the great trading ports of Calcutta, Madras and Bombay and handed them over to the care of friends and nurses to be taken home. Such separations were one of the saddest aspects of the Raj, almost sadder than the terrible toll that heat and disease took yearly from the British who lived in India. Sadder still was that every mother expected to loose three children out of every five that she bore. India was littered with the graves of their children.

Emily rejoined her father in Delhi in 1848 at the age of sixteen after spending her childhood in England. Her mother had died while she was in England. Her father who was a Delhi Resident, died in mysterious circumstances from some subtle poison in 1853. Her brother, Theophilus, was Chief Magistrate in Delhi at the outbreak of the mutiny in 1857. He made a miraculous escape to Hansi in a disguise supplied by his Indian friends.

In 1848, Edward Clive Bayley of the Bengal Civil Service arrived at Metcalfe House. He was twenty-seven and very shy. His and Emily's eyes met and it was a case of love at first sight. Years later, as an old woman Emily recalled what she was wearing when she met him for the first time. It was 'an embroidered white muslin with three flounces and a blue sash'.

Edward seized every chance to visit the Metcalfes in Delhi and as a proper Victorian suitor said nothing of his feelings to Emily until November 1849. He was offered the post of undersecretary in the foreign department which meant that he would be stationed in Simla for at least three years and able to provide a wife with a comfortable house and a good climate.

Emily married Edward in March 1850 and travelled up to Simla to live with her husband at a house that is still here, the Priory. Unlike many others Emily married for love.

The couple also fell in love with Simla. They spent twenty-eight years of togetherness and happiness here. They took long walks on the narrow roads and forest paths in the surrounding hills. As M.M. Kaye recalled, '... never to miss the experience to wake at dawn and to see from one's window the long line of the Himalayas spanning in the horizon and to watch the peaks catch fire one after another as the sun comes up. To see the enormous stretch of the plains at the evening when the smoke from the cooking fires draws out like long blue veils and the cattle comes straggling back from the grazing grounds and every cane brake is full of fireflies. To watch the enormous Indian moon lift slowly up though the dusty green twilight to glimmer on marble domes and minarets and carved temples which were old when Elizabeth-I was young. To stroll through the colour and clamours of the bazaars. Listen to Sitars and Tom-Toms and to smell the scent of jasmine and frangi-pani and water on hot dry ground. We who were born to all this and lived and loved all this can truthfully say that our lives were indeed "fallen on to us in pleasant places".'

The Governor-General Lord Dalhousie and his wife were very kind to Emily and Edward and took the newly weds on a long trek through the Simla Hills.

Emily gives a lyrical description of the hill country beyond Simla. Towards the end of this trip Emily became unwell and by October when they returned to Simla and the Priory she was in such poor health that a certain Doctor Hay reported her to be 'very ill – too ill to remain in India. She was to be sent to England as early as possible'; in spite of her grief and dismay at the prospect of being parted from Edward, a passage was booked for her on a ship sailing from Calcutta in the second week of December.

Her luggage had already been packed and sent on ahead and she was due to depart that very night when she writes, 'We were startled by the birth our first child.' Apparently, it had never occurred to anyone that there might be a perfectly ordinary explanation for her 'illness' – least of all to Emily. Her own mother had been dead many years ago. All the same Edward must have been pretty dim not to have noticed anything odd and he cannot have improved matters by fainting when 'the doctor told him of the event that had taken place.' When he finally came to, he rushed out-see if he could get any warm clothing for his new-born daughter. He returned with an 'exquisitely embroidered cambric robe and a pink plush cloak!!'.

No doubt, the passage to England was cancelled and after that there was no more talk of ill-health. Emily left Himachal with her husband (by now, Sir Edward) only after his retirement in 1878, after three lovely decades here. She lost two of the thirteen children that she bore. But the story of the birth of their first child always brought a smile to her lips. And, many times she laughed alone when she remembered the passage to England that had to be called off.

1831

3

When Rani Became A Boy

The Raja of Kapurthala – Jagatjit Singh – was eleven years old when the members of the court decided to find him his first wife. Traditionally, it was a suitable age. That the boy weighed 130 kg was not a problem but to find a bride was. It was not easy to trace girls of high pedigree.

A large group of courtiers travelled to the Kangra Valley, some 200 km from Kapurthala, in search of a girl of Rajput origin. They desired a union that would strengthen links with the great families of Rajputana.

With them went professional drum beaters, announcing the search from village to village. They read out the preconditions related to caste, lineage and age. Parents came with their girls and each girl was examined and some of the courtiers took this duty to such meticulous extremes, there were complaints about their zeal. Normally, the royal advisers chose the bride out of more than 250 girls.

Originally, Jagatjit's family had belonged to the mediocre caste of the *Kalal* who in olden times were in charge of brewing alcohol for the royal houses. Jassa Singh, a brilliant forbear, helped by the Sikhs, was able to bring together an army, rise up and unify Kapurthala. But the stigma of the *Kalal* still weighed on some members of the court. Did a Punjabi proverb not say 'Crow, *kalal* and dog, do not trust them even when they are asleep'? For that reason it was important to secure the bloodline.

The courtiers from Kapurthala came with arrogance, given the fact that they represented a prince, howsoever fat he was. They knew there would be many takers. For that reason, it was necessary to verify the girls' antecedents and no member of the retinue was allowed to accept bribes in order to include a young girl who was not appropriate.

They chose a beautiful girl of the same age as the Rajah, who later assumed the title of Her First Highness Harbans Kaur. She had big, dark eyes, and her skin was as golden as wheat. They negotiated the terms of her dowry with her parents, which would be made effective at the time of the marriage, set for 16 April 1886, when the young couple reached the worthy age of fourteen.

After a few years, Jagatjit Singh himself went to Kangra Valley to select his second wife. He had grown up, was still fat, and was interested in finding someone he could share his life with. He wrote in his diary, 'At present, an educated Indian feels the need to have an intelligent wife in his home, capable for her qualities and personal achievements of being a worthy companion to share his joys and sorrows.'

He not only found himself a wife but someone with whom he fell in love when he saw her for the first time. She was Rani Kanari – a gay, sophisticated woman. She too belonged to the Kangra Valley, like his first wife. She was a Rajput from a rich lineage but with no fortune.

Jagatjit found her different from the others. Kanari was not the prototype submissive Indian woman like Harbans Kaur, his first wife. She had a personality of her own and a sense of humour, although she spoke no English and had never been out of the Kangra Valley.

One meeting was adequate for Jagatjit Singh to fall deeply in love with her. He proposed marriage to her.

In Rani Kanari he discovered the kind of wife he was in search of and he was not wrong. Kanari would in fact prove to be much more than that. She was not only beautiful but bold, courageous, adventurous and intelligent.

Jagatjit Singh was educated and very much influenced by the liberal, Anglophile education he had received. Indian women could satisfy him sexually or could be the mothers of his children, but it was not easy to find one to share all aspects of his life with. So, at the dawn of the twentieth century, his dream of finding a woman capable of being a wife and friend at the same time, and able to move in both worlds, the East and the West, with the same ease as he did was fulfilled by Rani Kanari. She was unlike other women who were content to live in the *zenana* and hardly took part in their husband's social life.

When Jagatjit Singh had to go to England and Europe he was determined to take Rani Kanari with him. He wanted to have fun and share the good times with her. But he came up against absolute resistance on the part of the British authorities. Alluding to matters of protocol, they did not authorise him to travel with any of his Ranis, not even with Her First Highness Harbans Kaur. Jagatjit Singh did not like the high-handed attitude of the British authorities. He started to think of a plan to take Rani Kanari with him.

There was an ongoing tussle between the representatives of the Crown and the rulers of the Indian states. The Rajas felt that the British Residents and others needlessly interfered in their private affairs, whereas the British seized every opportunity to reprimand the rulers of their inappropriate and unbecoming behaviour. Raja Jagatjit Singh had been severely reprimanded the previous year for 'inappropriate behaviour' in Simla, for allowing himself to be led on by his friend – the Rajah of Dholpur. They procured tribal girls from the mountains by buying them from their impoverished and helpless families. This had provoked abundant correspondence between Colonel Henderson of the garrison in Lahore and Sir James Lyall, his ex-tutor.

But Raja Jagatjit Singh was determined to take Rani Kanari on the trip by any means, 'just in case his sperm went bad'. He chose not to request the imperial government but hatched a secret plan as he finalised the preparations for the journey.

'Hundreds of my subjects lined both sides of the road to wish me a good journey, and showed all the signs of sadness at my temporary absence,' he wrote in his diary on the day of his departure. From Bombay he embarked on the steamer *Thames*, which sailed at nightfall. 'My people never tired of explaining the ship, admiring the cleanliness and perfect tidiness of everything, observing the workings of the complicated machinery, new to them, and wondering how a ship so large could find its way at sea with no land in sight to guide the sailors . . . .'

His companions, the doctor, Lieutenant-Colonel Massy, the ministers, etc., received a huge shock when, in the private lounge of the Rajah's suite on board, they were met by a woman dressed in a grand sari. It was Rani Kanari. They immediately recognised her as one of the three attendants who had embarked on the journey. The Rajah had tricked everyone in order to get his own way. He had transformed his Rani into boy.

Disguised as a Sikh servant, Rani Kanari had slipped by. As in those days there were no individual passports, the trick had worked. The only one who could ruin the plan was Lieutenant-Colonel Massy, but the Rajah knew he would not. Massy, who had been one of his tutors, respected him and considered himself his friend. Besides, he saw it as yet another one of the twenty-one-year-old prince's wicked tricks. He thought he was rather capricious, but a good fellow deep down.

They stopped in Egypt, then England, France, and finally, the United States. The Rajah attended the London wedding of the Duke of York without his wife, who remained in their suite at the Savoy Hotel – his second home, as he would call it – passing off her boredom with gin-fizz, a drink that began to be popular at the time. One day later, from one of the suite's balconies, they were able to see a demonstration in the street in favour of the independence of Ireland, which reminded the Rajah of '. . . the artificial agitation that has begun recently in India at the orders of the Congress Party', as he wrote in his diary. 'These demonstrations remind me of a bottle of soda water which, when opened, is strong, then almost immediately loses gas and then becomes insipid.'

In England Rani Kanari was always disguised as a servant, but then, once they had crossed the English Channel, they relaxed as she took on her role as wife more and more often, dressing as elegantly as European women.

In a group photo they had taken in Paris, the Raja is seated with his scepter in his hand, wearing a light-coloured silk coat, trousers, a wide tie and a salmon-pink turban. The surprise element in the photograph is of the person sitting on a chair next to the Rajah, a young woman with fine features, wearing a long-sleeved satin dress of European style and cut.

The trip lasted eight months. On his return the Raja was received by the Military Secretary of the Governor of Bombay on behalf of the Viceroy of India. The Maharani remained unnoticed as she was again disguised as a boy.

This is how the duo in love fooled the British authorities.

1893

4

Scandal Point

Today, Scandal Point on the Mall Road in Shimla is a popular meeting place. 'I will meet you at Scandal Point,' is perhaps the most uttered line by a Shimalite. If you ask about the story behind this peculiar and distinctive name you get to hear different versions. Most popular is that the Maharaja of Patiala eloped with his lady love from here on a horseback and took her to Chail. Some say that the damsel was the daughter of the Viceroy while others say that she was the wife of a high ranking army officer. Images of a young, tall, handsome maharaja galloping away with a blonde beauty in white, followed by British and Indian swordsmen chasing them, flash in the mind. There is no historical record of such a bizarre happening, yet the myth and legend of Scandal Point lives on.

But there are several other authentic historical records which transport us back to a time full of gaiety, fun, frolic, love affairs, little summer flings and nuanced romances in this summer capital of the Raj.

Diwan Jeewan Dass, Minister of the Raja of Kapurthala has recorded his personal experiences about this time. He writes that from the beginning of the World War-I in 1914 up to the end of World War-II in 1945, Simla, Dalhousie and other hill-stations had become the summer resorts of British officers and their families as well as of the ruling Indian princes and their families. 'The whole atmosphere of these summer resorts was nothing but gaiety, frivolity and sex indulgence.' Kipling has also chronicled the frivolity of affairs and alliances during these times in his writings.

There were a number of alliances between Indian maharajas and European women. Some of these men married European women while others preferred them as their mistresses. They lived with them publicly in England, Europe and America. Some even lived with them in their palaces in total disregard of their legitimate consorts. They bought houses, chateaus and villas in England, France and other places where they spent their summer vacations with their European wives or mistresses, and entertained their friends. Everywhere in the big hotels in London, Paris, Berlin, New York and other capitals of the world, huge receptions and dinner parties were arranged by these maharajas and princes and these were attended by their European or American mistresses and the cream of society in world capitals.

The aspiration of Indian maharajas and princes to marry a British, European or American woman was checked by the succession law that stated that sons born out of such alliances would not inherit the throne. This law was a great curb on the rulers of the Indian States. The European women realised that they were not gainers in marrying Indian rulers and preferred to remain as their mistresses with dignified titles bestowed upon them by the maharajas which were recognised by the government. Many times Lord Curzon denied permission to Indian princes and maharajas to travel to England and Europe.

The parties and balls organised by rich Indian maharajas in Shimla were very popular, particularly fancy dress balls which could be attended in disguise. Diwan Jarmani Dass remembered that, 'Printed dance cards were issued to the participants before the ball to make reservations for dancing, and it was very seldom that British women refused the invitation of an Indian to dance and to reserve dances for him in their dance cards. While dancing was going on, dozens of couples would disappear into the park and miss their dancing reservations. After the ball, the maharajas, maharanis, princesses, society ladies, high British military officers, civilians, Indians holding high positions in the government, and their consorts and relatives, had to ride in rickshaws pulled by porters in magnificent uniforms.'

The wealth and prosperity of Indian princes and maharajas always fascinated the British. While the men were intrigued and envied their lavish lifestyle, the ladies were willing to go to any extent to look at the diamonds and jewels possessed by the kings and other royals. Indian style with precious stones, gems and diamonds woven into clothes with rich embroidery mesmerised them. It is interesting that though Lady Curzon ordered her state trousseau from Worth of Paris she had her clothes embroidered in India according to local patterns.

European jewellers from London, Paris and Amsterdam set out on long sea voyages in the hope of doing business with the princes. They could wait for months without seeing a maharaja but would be taken on tiger-shoots and sightseeing around marble temples in Rolls-Royces. 'Diamonds,' sniffed one observer on the Prince of Wales's tour in 1875, 'seem as plentiful in India as blackberries in England.'

The Maharajas of Kapurthala and Patiala were handsome Sikhs with their black beards tucked under turbans held with ruby, diamond and sapphire *torahs*. Kapurthala's Maharaja Jagatjit Singh's favourite was a clip of three thousand diamonds and pearls winking in his tea-rose-pink turban, while on his belt he wore a huge deep-golden topaz, one of the biggest in the world. The Maharaja of Patiala was even more striking. He was six feet tall, and had a preference for a daffodil yellow or jet black turban held with a cluster of emeralds. He tended to wear white buckskins, a long tunic of scarlet trimmed with gold and thigh-high black leather boots. On a ceremonial day in Delhi, he would not be wearing less than four ropes of pearls at his waist, and the fashion was to string emerald beads between each pearl. He wore a belt of diamonds, and a gold lame scarf that was held by a four-inch emerald. Five necklaces of diamonds and emeralds were tiered round his neck with a collar of diamonds in platinum at the top. He carried a jewelled sword.

Several English ladies viewed the bedecked Indian rulers with awe and longing. And the Indian rulers loved to have a relationship with them. A popular strategy to capture the hearts of British women was horses. They loved riding horses and as hired horses in hill stations were of very poor breed and physique, British women avoided them. The good horses were not available except in the stables of the maharajas.

Maharaja Jagatjit Singh was enthralled by a beautiful English woman and invited her many times for dinners and balls. She accepted his invitations gladly, but when it came to flirtation, or dining with the Maharaja alone, she made one excuse or the other and the Maharaja was disappointed. One evening, he told her that he would send her two horses for riding and that she could go for riding excursions with her boyfriend. She was indeed very pleased. After a few days when she and her boyfriend had got used to riding these beautiful horses, the Maharaja stopped sending them. The lady came begging for the loan of the horses and in return agreed to consider the Maharaja's proposal which was to have supper with him alone.

The English thought that Maharaja Jagatjit Singh was a 'womaniser' and together with Maharaja Rajinder Singh of Patiala and the Raja of Dholpur, the three had a reputation of being 'extravagant' hooligans, as they were described by an English officer. But the fact that they were criticised in secret reports did not mean that they were excluded from

British society. Quite the opposite because all said and done, they were blue-blooded. The Maharaja of Jaipur called the Queen of England by her pet name, Lizzy, and the three 'hooligans' rubbed shoulders with the cream of society, becoming the favoured company of the new Viceroy, Lord Curzon and his wife.

The Maharaja of Patiala, Rajinder Singh (1872–1900) had three houses in Shimla (located near each other) – Oakover (now the official residence of the Chief Minister of Himachal), Cedar (Punjab Government's guest house in Shimla) and Rookwood (a private property). He was given the title Farzand-e-Khas-Daulat-e-Englishia, meaning the most favourite son of the English empire by the British, and he entertained the high and mighty of the empire in these houses.

But this partying and festivity came to an abrupt end when an incident shook the Viceroy and he took the decision of banishing the three princes from the limits of Simla. The incident set Simla society ablaze with gossip and rumours. Thus, the legend of Scandal Point was born and the spot reverberates with juicy stories, authentic and not so authentic, till date. It happened one night at Oakover . . . .

The three Maharajas invited Lady Curzon to Oakover to see their jewels. The Lady tried on a pearl necklace insured by Lloyd's for a million dollars, and a tiara made of a thousand and one blue and white diamonds. 'These jewels look better with a sari,' Rajinder Singh said to her and then, 'Why don't you try this one which belonged to my grandmother?'

Lady Curzon ended up wrapped in a red sari embroidered in gold thread, wearing the jewels, pearl necklaces and tiara including the legendary Eugene diamond. She looked pretty, an oriental queen. Rajinder Singh suggested a photograph as a souvenir. So, she was photographed by the famous pioneer of photography in India, Lala Deen Dayal who was staying there as a guest.

Not only did the Viceroy get to know of this, the picture got printed in British taboloids. The wife of the Viceroy dressed as a maharani! Having dinner with the three womanisers!

Lord Curzon was so angry that he forbade the three princes to visit Simla without his permission. Maharaja Rajinder Singh reacted by enjoying his parties at his own summer capital at Chail, sixty kilometres from Simla at an altitude of three thousand metres, higher than Simla.

What a scandal! Simla was abuzz with gossip and more gossip.

1898–1902

5

The Princess

The six–year-old princess was on the verge of tears as her father and brothers made their way across the courtyard, laughing and joking. They were going to Simla town without her. She had to stay back at Newland, their temporary home. She too wanted to see the city of *sahibs* and *memsahibs*, of rajas and ranis, of fun and festivity. She wept inconsolably for sometime but then she took a decision and stopped weeping. She watched from the balcony as they walked toward the magic city she could not see, she felt defeated but she promised herself that someday she would not only see Simla, but the whole world. The little girl clenched her fists on the railing and bit her lips to keep back the tears. She never expected that this pledge to herself will be fulfilled.

The child was Brinda, Princess of Jubbal, a hill state near Simla. She was the daughter of the brother of Raja of Jubbal. She was born on a chilly January morning as the snow tumbled about the Himalayan mountains. Her mother, who had married at eleven and borne two children before her – both of whom died in infancy – was just fourteen year old.

Their family had ruled the state of Jubbal for over thirty generations. The family belonged to one of the thirty-six Rajput clans who claimed descent from Sun, Moon, or Sacred Fire. Some records reveal that her ancestors came from Central Asia in the fifth century and married into Hindu families. Kingdom of Jubbal, about 80 kilometres from Simla, was established about the year 1066 after the invasion by the Muslims.

As was the custom in those days, her marriage was arranged by her parents when she was just seven years old. Her husband-to-be was the eldest son and heir of the state of Kapurthala, Paramjit Singh. The Prince was nine years old at that time. It was a time when child marriage was the norm. These marriages were consummated the moment both were physically capable, some even before the bride reached puberty. But Brinda's father-in-law, Maharaja Jagatjit Singh thought otherwise. She recalls this in her memoirs, 'The Tika Raja and I were to remain apart, receive our education, and marry at an appropriate age. My future was to be in the hands of his father, the Maharaja of Kapurthala, who would direct my education and upbringing. In other words, he was now my guardian. It was the end of my carefree childhood.'

Brinda was sent to Paris at the age of ten for education and she stayed with a French family (Pracomtals), friends of her would-be father-in-law. She was sixteen when she fell in love with a French boy. She describes this tale in a poignant manner in her memoirs. Her story has drama, pathos and romance. It is a tale of love and longing which remained unfulfilled . . . .

ଔ

'. . . I fell in love for the first time with a young French boy. It was bound to happen. An impressionable young girl caught in the romantic atmosphere of that time would almost certainly find her first love among the young people she was growing up with.

I had known him for some time as a friend of the Pracomtals. His name was not Guy but I shall call him that because even today there are a few friends who knew how much we cared for each other those many years ago.

First love is much the same for everyone, and I, too, was convinced that only a miracle had crossed our lives together. Guy told me about the lovely French fable which says that before two people are born their soul is split in heaven and one part goes to a man and the other half to a woman. If the two souls find each other on earth they have perfect happiness together but if they do not, all through their lives they must search in order to assuage the loneliness which comes from being incomplete.

We both believed it, as lovers almost always do, and we felt complete and safe for the first time in our lives. My aching loneliness was replaced by the magic of a dream, of gazing in wonder at the face of my beloved with astonishment that love like that could have happened to me.

Guy was an officer in the army but I saw him at balls and parties when he was home on leave. One evening as we were waltzing together at a ball given by the Comtesse de Fels, he guided me behind a pillar where he told me, as the dancers whirled by us, that he loved me and wanted to marry me.

Until that moment I had thought of Guy only as a fantasy I could never achieve. After all, I was already engaged and, more important, it never occurred to me that he would be interested in me.

I turned pale as he told me of his love. 'You can't mean it,' I whispered. 'It's too impossible.'

He looked at me with his blue eyes which shone like the sea and knit his golden eyebrows together.

'I do love you,' he said gravely, 'and there is nothing I won't give up for you.'

'I cannot marry you,' I cried. 'You know I am already promised to someone else.'

With the passion of youth he seized me by the shoulders and nearly shouted aloud in the ballroom.

'If I cannot have you I have no interest in life,' he cried.

I tore out of his grasp. 'You must let me go,' I said, trying to hold back the tears.

Guy started after me as I fled from the ballroom. I hurried over to my guardian and asked to be taken home at once.

'My dear child,' she asked in concern when she saw my flushed face, 'is something wrong? Are you ill?'

'Yes,' I answered, and began to weep. 'I am ill and want to leave the ball.'

I went home immediately. But all night long I tossed fitfully in my bed. Guy's face spun about me in the dark room. He was everything I had ever dreamed about. Everything about him was infinitely familiar, like a love that was always destined to be a part of me. He was familiar as all the secret dreams of a person are. Finding him had been like finding myself.

Seeing Guy was like seeing sunshine for the first time. He was filled with laughter and smiles and gaiety. He had no melancholy about him at all. And his blondness made him glitter in my eyes like a magical god who had come from nowhere to find me. He was what my dreams had been all about.

But from the first I was aware that Guy could only be a dream. I was not European enough to give up everything for love – my Indian roots and training would not let me forget about my responsibilities so quickly.

But Guy was not so easily dissuaded. The day following the ball he appeared at the Pracomtals for tea, and the first chance he got to be alone with me in the garden he began to speak. 'If I could,' he said. 'I would marry you tomorrow. I am prepared for the difficulties.'

'Guy, why do you torture yourself like this – and me? It is impossible. I can never marry you.'

'When people love each other,' he answered me, walking up and down the garden path, 'there must be a way for them.'

Women are often wiser than men and although I was years younger than Guy, I knew even then that it is not always possible to have what you want out of life.

'Even if I were not engaged,' I said, 'you forget about the great differences between us.'

'There is no difference,' Guy answered angrily, 'between two people in love.'

'What about your family?' I asked. 'Europeans have such prejudices. It is one thing for your family to accept me socially; it is another to allow their only son to marry me.'

Guy turned red with anger. 'I can't let you speak that way,' he shouted. 'Who are we Europeans? What do we mean compared to a culture as old and fine as India?'

'It is useless to argue,' I answered sadly. 'That's the way the world is. We alone cannot expect it to change for us.'

'I cannot let you go,' he cried, 'it is too much to ask.'

'You have very little choice,' I said. 'You forget that I have my duty and I must return to India.'

But it was easier to answer Guy rationally than to assuage the terrible pain in my heart. How could I leave him when I loved him so? If I could marry Guy, I thought, life would be as I had always wanted it since coming to Europe. Nothing would change very much. I understood the ways of Europeans by then more than I could believe in my Indian background. I was too rebellious for India, too defiant to go back to a life where I would remain half-veiled physically and emotionally. There was no submission in me.

In the months that followed our declaration of love we tortured each other with terrible scenes. The agony was heightened by the fact that we could never be really alone. We saw each other frequently since we were constantly at the same parties and receptions, but in those days a solitary rendezvous was impossible. So, we snatched moments alone at parties and balls but never had but a few minutes before some interruption came to separate us.

Leaving out my own responsibilities, my judgement was quite correct about Guy's family. They were ardent Catholics and the marriage of their son to a Hindu, whom they considered a heathen, was unthinkable. I was alone in France. Despite the kindness and welcome shown to me in Europe, there was a vast difference between the two worlds. It was not expected that I would attempt to bridge it.

Guy wanted me to elope. 'We'll go to the registrar's office,' he said. 'And once it's done they'll just have to accept it.'

For days I was torn with indecision. Suddenly, the thought of returning to India to marry a man I did not know or understand was unbearable. And the time was galloping towards me when I would have to leave on the long journey across the black sea.

Guy even went to his grandmother, a kind, dear old lady who knew and loved me. She told him she would help him and give him the money to marry me.

So, it could be possible after all. The real barrier left was me. I was sick with conflict. I could not eat or sleep and each time the doorbell rang I jumped with nervousness. I had to talk to someone. But there was no one to talk to.

Finally, one night Yolande, elder daughter of Pracomtals came to me. 'Everyone is talking about you,' she said.

My heart leaped in terror. 'You look so ill,' she said. 'They want to know what's the matter with you. Can't you tell me?'

I sank back on the bed in relief. Then I began to sob with exhaustion and all the pent-up emotions I had kept inside me for so many months. I decided to tell Yolande everything.

Yolande's viewpoint was harsh but practical. 'There is no future in such a romance,' she said. 'Give him up at once and forget about him. You could not be happy together if all around you, you had created misery.'

The following day I saw Guy and told him that we must forget each other. An emotional scene followed, with both of us weeping and torn apart over the agony of separation. But when we parted nothing had been settled.

That night in my pain I did something I had never done before. I prayed, not to the gods of Hinduism but to the Holy Virgin of the Christians, holding in my hands a picture which the Comtesse d'Eu had given me years before.

I woke hours later after a dream. My mother, looking as she had the last time I saw her, had come to me and said, 'A Rajput cannot go back on her word. You must be married as you promised. This man is an untouchable; if you marry him you will be a woman without country or race and all your family will share your disgrace.'

'Perhaps, it was my own conscience talking. But it filled me with a determination and resolve I had been incapable of before. The next day I told Guy of my dream and he knew finally that there was no longer any hope. But I could never stop loving him. He was often in my thoughts.'

※

Brinda returned to India and married Raja Paramjit Singh. When she returned to Paris after five years, she met Guy again.

She recalls in her memoirs . . . 'It had been more than five years since our last meeting but when we were together it was almost as if we had never been apart. From inside his army jacket he took out a golden coin I had given him years before. "I may go into battle any day now," he said soberly, "but I will always keep this with me as part of you." My eyes filled with tears as we said goodbye. He kissed my hand once tenderly and I watched his blond head disappear out of the door. I never saw him again. But years later, his brother came to see me to give me back the worn Indian coin. They had taken it from Guy's body as he lay on the field of battle in 1916.'

Brinda's love for Guy remained throughout her life. It was this love that made her change the course of her daughter Ourmila's life. She was instrumental in making her marry the man she loved.

The wish that Brinda made as a child to see the world was fulfilled and she travelled extensively in Europe and America. Her journey came to an end in Shimla where she died in 1970.

1910

6

Amrita Sher-Gil

Place: Summer Hill, Simla. Time: September 1935.

Malcolm Muggeridge was getting ready to leave India to join *Evening Standard* in London. He was flooded with strange emotions. His stay of a few months in Simla was one of the most memorable periods of his life so far. And all this was because of her. She was pure magic, an enigma.

Amrita came to see him off early morning – a most unusual time for her to be up and about. They sat on the wrought iron benches at the Summer Hill railway station for some time. Then, Amrita got up and started to walk along the rail track as Malcolm watched her. After a while she came up to him and took his hand and they walked up and down the platform together in the crisp September air.

They were speaking in French – 'an affectation' that they practised. She said, 'We'd had some *beaux* (fine) moments together, but also some moments *noir* (black*)*.'

This was true, Malcolm thought, and he was lost in memories of their time together.

He was sure she had a strong narcissistic trait in her. Once he had told her, 'You are really a virgin, because you have never experienced the spiritual equivalent of copulation; you have had many lovers but they'd left no scar. I will leave a scar,' She had laughed heartily at his assertion.

A wry smile crossed his lips as he recalled this conversation.

He was jolted back to the present at the sound of a rumble. It was time for him to say goodbye and get into the little mountain train. Through the carriage window they went on talking until with a shrill whistle, the train began to move.

Muggeridge continued to look out of the window, waving, until she was out of sight. The train had entered a tunnel. Amrita was left behind at the station. He knew that he would never see her again. His heart ached at the thought. His premonition came true too soon. Six years later, he heard that she'd died somewhat mysteriously when she was only twenty-eight years old. Later, he heard that her mother had taken her own life.

'Neither death surprised me,' he recorded in his diary.

Amrita Sher-Gil was no ordinary lady. Her persona was such that anyone who ever met her or even those who never met her, had a captivating story to tell. Most of the stories were woven around her insatiable hunger for men. She has been described as a nymphomaniac who 'is said to have given appointments to her lovers at two hours interval before she retired for the night.' Fact or fiction, Amrita was more than that; she was a great painter. Her claim that, 'Europe belongs to Picaso, Matisse and many others, India belongs only to me,' was not without merit.

As the train emerged from the tunnel, the small box-like compartment was filled with light and Muggerridge thought about the stories spreading in Simla circles about her. While some might have been true there were others that were pure concoction . . . invented by men and women who were jealous of her.

Amrita had set Simla society on fire. Men longed for her and women burnt with jealousy. Whenever she entered a room all conversation ceased as everyone turned to look at her . Once when Amrita 'slim, petite and svelte', dressed in a 'brilliant green sari with a flaming red blouse, wearing heavy Tibetan ear rings' entered Devicos, a popular restaurant in Simla, everyone was stunned into silence and stared at her as she glided past them.

While every man in Simla circles was drawn to her charms, Amrita herself clearly felt drawn to men who in some way stood outside the mainstream and critiqued it. These men, like her, lived on society's edge, refusing to accept conventional norms and opposing hypocrisy.

Malcolm Muggeridge was one such man who charmed Amrita. He was thirty-two, ten years older than Amrita, when he met her. At that time he was someone who, 'saw himself as a discarded product of a diseased civilisation, believing nothing, hoping for nothing, fearing nothing except the consciousness of my own melancholy.' This attracted Amrita towards him.

Malcolm saw Amrita at Sipi fair at Mashobra near Simla. He mentioned the meeting in his diary, dated 22 May 1935: 'All the while there was something exciting me. I'd seen a woman at Sipi Fair, half-Hungarian and half-Indian, beautiful in a way, wearing an exquisite sari. Warden, a Parsee, had introduced me to her, and had asked if I'd join them both at the Cecil Hotel dance. This was in my mind. I smelt emotional entanglement. Already it has affected me to the extent of not being able to write easily to Kit (his wife, based in London) – the first time for many weeks. In the evening (I) changed, took a brandy, danced with Hungarian – Indian several times, cemented our attraction, made her promise to ring me up. She is very sensual and made up, was wearing an exquisite silver and black sari, is rather self-consciously arty, has studied art in Paris; paints. We danced a Waltz. I said 'I'd like to dance and dance till I swooned.'

Amrita seems to have been stimulated and excited by Muggeridge as well, for in a letter to her sister Indira she wrote: 'I have met an extraordinary Englishman of whom Mummy has undoubtedly written to you and of whom consequently you must have the most utter misconception! He is really one of the most interesting, fascinating remarkable people I have ever met. Barring Marie Louise whom fundamentally he immensely resembles, I have never met anybody like him. (This feeling is entirely reciprocated)

And among this dull, uninteresting and scandal mongering crowd, we are an intense relief to one another.'

Amrita loathed the scandalmongers of Simla society and lived in her own world. She wrote to Karl (Khandalavala) in September 1937: 'You are right though, when you say that I live too much in a sequestered world of my own, but the fault I am inclined to think lies not so much in me as in people I meet and my surroundings. If you know the type of biped that inhabits social Simla you wouldn't blame me. Besides, returning into my shell mentally is my only defense against the onslaught of the mediocre thoughts that infest this place . . . . I have just completed a lovely sugary self-portrait that will make the public mouth water. I did it as a bait for future sitters.'

Malcolm Muggeridge leaned towards the window of the train for a last glimpse of Simla town as they neared Tara Devi station. As a reporter it was his business to be interested in everything. He had read with interest that the first sketches of the Simla – Kalka track were made in November 1847 and that it was constructed after more than fifty years. Bhalku a local villager was instrumental in laying the line. He found it amusing that this symbol of the power of the British Raj had to rely on the judgement of an illiterate old fakir called Bhalku. The track opened for public in 1906. He felt uneasy at the thought that the ninety-six-kilometre long journey from Simla to Kalka would take him through 103 tunnels and over 969 bridges. As the toy train slowly chugged out of Tara Devi station Malcolm saw the last vistas of the summer

Capital of the Raj. He took out his diary to pen down his thoughts but instead started to read his earlier notes . . . many of these were about Amrita.

Muggeridge had kept a detailed record of his relationship with Amrita. True to his nature he was absolutely objective about her drawbacks, yet able at the same time to stay deeply involved with her. He wrote on 6 June 1935: '. . . Sometimes I hate Amrita. Today for instance, I went out to meet her. She was sitting reading tattered love letters, letters which began 'Amrita!' Another 'Maintenant je suis soldat.' She said: 'This morning I went for a walk with Warden and he asked if he might kiss the tips of my fingers.' I get a sense of someone entirely egocentric, coarse, petulantly spoilt, almost to the point of physical nausea.

'We talked, both rather showing off. Every time she kissed me she re-rouged her lips, carefully shaping the colours on them to hump up in the middle.'

He also wrote in detail about a day spent with Amrita when, to his irritation, her mother ('an extremely vulgar, Hungarian Jewess') accompanied them.

On 16 June 1935 he wrote, '. . . she came at eight, in a green sari with a gold and red border. She talked about her lovers, her terrible obsession with herself very apparent. Then, she took off her jewels and let down her hair. It was like a third performance of a marvellous play, all the fascination, the sense of wonder, remains; all the same, you realise that though you might like to see it ten or twenty more times, there'll come a time when you don't want to see it anymore, when it'll be wearisome.'

'Amrita had her studio there, and I sat for her; or rather lolled on a sofa, sometimes reading, or just watching with fascination the animal intensity of her concentration, making her short of breath, with beads of sweat appearing on the faint moustache on her upper lip. It was this animality which she somehow transferred to the colours as she mixed them and splashed them on her canvas.'

'The pleasure of her company – and also at times the fatigue – lay in her vivid, forceful, direct reactions to life; the moral equivalent of her taste for steaks that were almost raw, and curries that were almost on fire.'

ଓ

Amrita was the elder of two daughters of a part-Jewish Hungarian mother, Marie Antoniette Gottesmann, and a Sikh father, Umrao Singh Sher-Gil, a widower with children from his first wife. He came from a distinguished, aristocratic family owning farmland, many houses and a large sugar mill at Saraya in Uttar Pradesh. But Marie, a hard-headed, eccentric woman interested in the fine arts and music, readily espoused the long-bearded and be-turbaned sardar under the impression that he was a very wealthy landowner, only to find that he in fact drew a measly pension from his family and was deeply involved in studying ancient Sanskrit and Persian texts and spent long hours watching stars at night. It was a miss-alliance from the start: she cheated on him, having affairs that came her way. It remained so till she shot herself in the head with his shotgun in their Simla home on 31 July 1948.

Both Amrita and her sister Indira were born in Budapest, were baptised as Roman Catholics and spent the first years of their lives there. At a very early age, Amrita took to drawing pictures, and Indira to playing the piano. From childhood Amrita was a serious, introvert girl who read a lot and preferred the company of adults to those of her own age. At Simla, she studied at the Convent of Jesus and Mary but was expelled from school because she rebelled at the school's compulsory mass attendance.

In Simla, Amrita and her sister participated in plays at the Gaiety Theatre. A local newspaper of 10 September 1924 speaks of the Sher-Gil sisters being well-trained and performing creditably in the two most difficult dances of the evening; one a Hungarian dance and the other in *God Pan and the Girl Who Lost Her Way in the Woods*. From Simla the family moved to Paris where the sisters pursued their studies, one in painting, the other in music. Amrita won recognition at the Ecole des Beaux Arts. Around then she grew conscious of her good looks.

Amrita never liked Europe and she returned to India. She stayed at Summer Hill in her father's house, The Holme. Karl Khandalavala, a noted art critic in Bombay, and fellow Hungarian Charles Fabri, who lived in Lahore, acclaimed her as perhaps the greatest painter of the century. Later, Amrita married Victor Egan, her cousin.

In Simla she enjoyed the colours of nature and loved to breathe fresh mountain air. Many times when she started for the Cecil or for Devicos in the rickshaw pulled by uniformed men, she stopped at the Rain Shelter between Summer Hill and the Cecil to look at the rolling hills. She loved mountain colours. The evening sky charmed her and fired her imagination.

She wrote in Simla in 1935, 'In Europe I felt that I have to go away from this kind of greyness and from this strange light in order to be able to breathe. Here everything is natural. In Europe the colours are different and the greyness and coldness of big cities I was never able to enjoy. There, I was not natural and honest because I was born with a certain thirst for colour and in Europe the colours are pale – everything is pale. Because we cannot paint in the West as we paint in the East – the colour of the white man is different from the colour of the Hindu and the sunshine changes the light. The white man's shadow is bluish purple while the Hindu has a golden-green shadow. Mine is yellow. Van Gogh was told that yellow is the favourite colour of gods and that is right.'

She worked as a painter in Simla and she was pleased with her work. She wrote in February 1935, 'I am happy because today I have worked a lot. I am improving since I am back. I paint differently with more style and more naturally without any effort. Everything comes easily. I wouldn't be able to achieve this if I remained in Paris – my struggle towards style was not natural and I hated to force it. But something was choking me – I couldn't work with joy. Apart from two/three months I was spending in Veroce (Hungary) but now when I come out from the grayish smoke and deep grayish building, atmosphere which makes me suffer, to free nature where I can see colourful dresses and especially I don't see paintings and the painter. I can breathe, I can move and I can paint.'

Amrita was fair, petite, with large, searching eyes and full lips. She wore bright-coloured saris and large beaded jewellery. She was liberal in her use of cosmetics and doused herself in perfume. Her flamboyance attracted attention wherever she went.

In Simla, she was more often than not thrown into the company of the affluent, the maharajas and the civil servants who had summer homes in the hill town. Beautiful and charismatic, she was courted by many and plied with invitations for dinner parties. Her lifestyle did not, however, prevent her from working in a concentrated manner during the day.

Her reckless affairs led to many juicy stories floating about her. Badruddin Tyabji writes in his memoirs that one winter, when he was staying in Simla, he invited Amrita for dinner. He had a fire lit that evening and western classical music playing on his gramophone. He wasted the first evening talking about literature and music. He invited her again. Before he knew what was happening, Amrita simply took off her clothes and lay stark naked on the carpet. She did not believe in wasting time. One letter from Amrita to Nehru written on 6 November 1937 which remained in his collection provides a glimpse of their relationship: 'You are not hard; you have got a mellow face. I like your face. It is sensitive, sensual and detached at the same time.' Iqbal Singh whom she met in Simla and became her friend had asked her why she did not paint Nehru and she replied that she would never paint Nehru because 'he is too good looking.'

It is sad that her parents burnt all her letters including those written by Jawahar Lal Nehru. She wrote to them in 1938 with a sense of hurt, 'I must admit that it was a bit of a shock to hear that all my letters are being perused and consigned to the flames! . . . I merely hope that at least the letters of Marie Louise, Malcolm Muggeridge, Jawahar Lal Nehru, Edith and Karl have been spared . . . however now I suppose that I have to resign myself to a bleak old age, unrelieved by the entertainment that the perusal of old love letters would have afforded it.'

There is no doubt that Amrita Sher-Gil, a great artist, had an enigmatic and very colourful life.

1935

7

A Spiritual Bond: Edwina And Jawahar Lal Nehru

Edwina, Countess Mountbatten of Burma, was found dead on the morning of 21 February 1960 in her room in Borneo, Malaysia. She was lying on her bed, her body was cold. She had suffered a heart failure. One of the world's richest women, she had no grand possessions with her at the moment of her unexpected demise. There was only a pile of old letters on the bedside table. She must have been reading them, for they were strewn across her bed, as if they had fluttered from her hands when she died. These letters were from a very special friend – Jawahar Lal Nehru.

The previous morning she had been woken up by Robert Noel Turner, her host and Chief Secretary of North Borneo for a glimpse of Mount Kinabalu, the highest mountain in Malaysia which usually remained covered under mist. She was lucky to see the mountain just before it was enveloped moments later. Turner told her that the mountain was worshipped by, 'Dusuns who live on the lower slopes. They believe it is the resting place of the souls of the dead.'

She had arrived at Borneo on 18 February from India, via Malay and Singapore. She was in India to attend the Republic Day parade on 26 January 1960. During the day time she did her charity work and spent her evenings with Jawahar Lal Nehru.

Official biographers of Jawahar and Edwina believe that their affair had not begun till May 1948 when they had gone to Mashobra near Shimla. 1948 was a difficult time. India had gained Independence but Partition and riots had wounded her. Mahatma Gandhi's assassination had left Nehru deeply shaken and disillusioned. Edwina could sense his tension and exhaustion. She persuaded him to spend a few days up in the hills with her as they had the year before. Edwina later wrote to Nehru, '. . . getting you to Mashobra to talk naturally and informally had become an obsession.'

She prevailed upon him and Jawahar drove with Lord Mountbatten (whom he lovingly called Dickie), Edwina and their daughter Pamela to the Retreat at Mashobra in a red open-top car. The drive into the mountains from Delhi took several hours. The hot dusty plains of Punjab gave way to cool hillside tracks at the base of the Himalayas and then to thickly wooded slopes lightly veiled in the mist that lingers before the monsoon rains. Jawahar's mood began to lighten.

Dickie was fond of Jawahar and he was aware that he and his wife shared a special bond. He was also conscious of the very high political jeopardy that this relationship presented to him but he was sure that there was no personal risk. He knew that Edwina would never leave him for the Prime Minister of India. 'Please keep this to yourselves but she and Jawaharlal are so sweet together,' he wrote to his elder daughter Patricia. 'They really dote on each other in the nicest way and Pammy and I are doing everything we can to be tactful and help. Mummy has been incredibly sweet lately and we have been such a happy family.'

And so, Edwina and Jawahar walked together among the wild strawberry bushes during the days and in the evenings drove with Pamela along long winding roads to the brightly-lit roads of Simla. Dickie stayed behind at the house to devote himself to his work but this also gave his wife the space and privacy she always desired. She made the most of it. Edwina and Jawahar met early morning in the garden and then they drove together along the Tibet road, stopping to picnic in the woods. They stayed up late after Dickie and Pamela had retired to bed.

A decade later Jawahar would remind her about a sudden realisation at Mashobra. He wrote to Edwina on 12 March 1957 '. . . that there was a deeper attachment between us that some uncontrollable force of which I was only dimly aware drew us to each other.'

Being together at Mashobra round the clock heightened the intensity of their feelings which both exhilarated and frightened them. It was in Mashobra that they made a pact that their work would always have to come first. But it was a very difficult decision and both of them were aware of this.

Jawahar wrote to Indira, his daughter, about this time, 'I had four very restful and quiet days in Mashobra. I did no work at all although I took many papers. I was not in the mood to work.'

Edwina felt the same and did not want him to leave. She saw Jawahar off at half past six in the morning on the day he left Mashobra. She later wrote to him, 'I hated seeing you drive away this morning. You have left me with a strange sense of peace and happiness. Perhaps, I have brought you the same?' Jawahar replied as soon as he returned to Delhi, 'Life is a dreary business and when a bright patch comes it rather takes one's breath away.'

Both Edwina and Jawahar were very passionate and sensitive people. During the World War-II Edwina used to visit the hospitals in Europe. She always carried her make-up, a comb, a clothes brush and a shoe shine pad so that she looked her best. She inspected hygiene and organisational facilities and had a keen eye for nursing procedure and always spoke to every single patient in the hospital. Jawahar, at the same time, was deeply worried about communal tensions in India and his relationship with Edwina became more important when both went out into the streets of Delhi to deal with rioters. On one occasion, Edwina was with her friend, the Health Minister Amrit Kaur when they heard that Nehru

A SPIRITUAL BOND: EDWINA AND NEHRU | 53

had gone out alone. They found him attempting to stop a crowd of armed men. On another occasion, Jawahar heard of an attack planned on Jamia Milia Islamia University. At night the students fearing for their lives turned off their lamps and stood guard. They could hear splashes as Muslims from nearby villages were chased into the Jamuna river, pursued by mobs intent on drowning them. Without waiting to organise a bodyguard for himself Jawahar got into a taxi and drove alone through the treacherous countryside – only to find Edwina already there without guards, trying to pacify the mob.

Again and again, events brought the two together. Richard Symonds, a friend of Edwinas' who was working alongside her in Delhi and Punjab, noted the value of her friendship with Jawahar for relief effort. 'If we had problems where the PM's attention was needed,' he remembered, 'she had got it.'

Vivacious, chic and slim, at forty-five Edwina was still in her prime. Her position as one of the world's richest women had never made her happy. The heiress to millions had never been more content than when she was working in the hot, rough and filthy refugee camps set up across riot-scarred Punjab.

At the beginning of September 1947 Edwina noted in her diary her surprise at how deeply fond of Jawahar she had become. The feeling was mutual. In at least one photograph of the two of them visiting a refugee camp Jawahar's hand can be seen clasped protectively around Edwina's. Jawahar's niece Nayantara Pandit came to live with him in October and observed the relationship firsthand. 'It was a very deep emotional attachment, there is no doubt about that,' she remembered. 'I think it had all the poignance of the lateness of the hour . . . that terrible cutoff-ness from the world and anxieties about India, where are we going, all the rest of it and then to find this – and for her apparently also a great and unique love.'

Their friendship was a subject of gossip in Delhi society. Rumour had it that they were very much in love, and met on the journeys the Prime Minister of India made abroad.

It seemed Lord Mountbatten minded not at all. Leaders of the Indian freedom movement speculated about the impact of the Nehru–Edwina relationship on political matters. Maulana Abul Kalam Azad writes in *India Wins Freedom*, 'I have often wondered how Jawaharlal was won over by Lord Mountbatten. He is a man of principle but he is also impulsive and very amenable to personal influences. I think one factor responsible for the change was Lady Mountbatten. She is not only extremely intelligent but has most attractive and friendly temperament . . . .'

Nehru and Edwina wrote letters frequently to each other. When Edwina left for England after India gained Independence, they wrote daily, then once a week and finally they settled for once a month. These wonderful letters tell a unique tale of love, affection and bonding. Nehru and Edwina shared their lives with each other for twelve long years and a deep, pious and spiritual bond held them together. Their relationship might not have been physical but they loved each other deeply.

They seemed to fill the gap in each other's lives.

'Mr Nehru was obviously a very lonely man,' remembered Patricia Mountbatten, daughter of Edwina Mountbatten, 'and my mother was somebody who had not been able to communicate and make easy relationships with anybody, even with her own husband. I think that these two had the similar lack in their lives which the other person fulfilled which gave them a very strong relationship to each other.' The Mountbattens' other daughter, Pamela agreed. 'I have always been asked whether I think Nehru and my mother were in love. The answer undoubtedly is that yes they were.' In the same interview Lady Pamela Hicks made a point of stating that she did not believe the relationship to be physical.

Nobody can ever know the exact date and time when both of them started to feel strongly and passionately for each other but that they were destined to meet is certain. And their first meeting happened in the most extraordinary and remarkable manner! Nehru landed at Singapore on 18 March 1946 and met Lord Mountbatten at Government House. Nehru was to leave for his hotel when Mountbatten told him that his wife was keen to meet him and that she was at the YMCA for charity work. Nehru agreed to the change of plan. When they arrived at the YMCA, the Indians there clamoured for a glimpse of Nehru, their beloved leader. In the rush and raucous they lost Edwina. As Nehru was not very tall he stood up on a chair to look for her. He saw her trying to get out of the room by crawling on all fours! Indira Gandhi related the incident to Richard Hough, Edwina's biographer, 'Lady Mountbatten was flat on the floor when my father and she met in Singapore. When my father went in everyone rushed and they just knocked her down. So, the first thing they had to do, Lord Mountbatten and my father, was to rescue her and put her back on her feet.' 'It was an unusual introduction for us,' Nehru recalled later.

The fine looking man whom Edwina first met at floor level was soon to become the most important person in her life and to remain so till her death. Nehru became quite simply Edwina's first and only great love. He in turn had longed for a confidante and lover who would also keep his mind on edge and amuse him. Edwina's entry into his life was like a miracle, swift, bountiful and total, meeting all his needs. His daughter Indira emphasised that they 'were great friends . . . with the sort of life my father led it was a great relaxation for him to have someone quite different. They could discuss things intellectually and he was very fond of her.'

Dickie understood the relationship very well and he never felt that he was being kept in the dark. It was to her husband that Edwina entrusted the love letters from Jawahar following a hemorrhage. She had to undergo a dangerous surgery and felt that Dickie was the best person to keep those letters. She wrote to her husband while handing over this most prized possession, 'You will realise that these are a mixture of typical Jawahar letters, full of interest and facts and really historic documents. Some of them have no 'persona' remarks at all; others are love letters in a sense, though you yourself will realise the strange relationship – most of it spiritual – which exists between us. J has obviously meant a very great deal in my life in these last years and I think I in his. Our meetings have been rare and always fleeting but I think I understand him and perhaps he me as well as any human beings can ever understand each other.'

Dickie and Jawahar also exchanged letters. But they wrote to each other about Edwina more than anything else. They sent each other news of her achievements, updates on her activities, her over-work and her health.

After leaving India Edwina came back almost every winter for a few weeks. On one occasion she was due to visit Jawahar in Delhi but collapsed shortly before in Malta and nearly called the trip off on the doctor's advice. She concealed the extent of her illness but Dickie gave her a bland letter about politics to take to Jawahar, inside which he hid a five-page update on her condition. Edwina was desperate to go for Jawahar had promised her a visit to the Ajanta caves, the 2000-year-old Buddhist retreats. Edwina agreed to postpone her trip only after Jawahar sent her a telegram promising not to go to the caves without her. They finally went together in 1957.

The two men in Edwina's life were open with each other about their feelings. Dickie always emphasised that he would rather that Edwina 'should really get fit again and take things easy for as long as she likes' more than hurry back to him. Jawahar wrote sadly to Dickie of 'a certain emptiness' that struck him whenever Edwina left.

Destiny had woven India into the life of Edwina Mountbatten. It was in India that she was engaged to

Lord Mountbatten in 1922 in Delhi, on Valentine's Day. Mountbatten wrote in his diary, 'I danced one and two with Edwina; she had three and four with David (Prince of Wales) and the fifth dance we sat out in the sitting room when I asked her if she would marry me and she said she would.' He further writes, 'Edwina chose an old Indian ring from Schwaigers Art Gallery.'

It is life's irony that Edwina who was engaged to Lord Mountbatten in India and wore an Indian engagement ring developed a profound, relationship with an Indian who became the first Prime Minister of independent India and then died in Borneo after her last visit to India with letters from an Indian strewn around her.

Edwina had asked her husband to bury her in a 'sack at sea'. H.M.S. Wakeful was offered by the Admiralty and sailed from Portsmouth. The coffin was discharged into the waves from beneath a Union Jack. Mountbatten was in tears as he kissed a wreath of flowers before throwing it into the sea.

Nehru's last act on behalf of the woman he loved was to order an Indian warship to accompany as escort the British frigate in which Edwina's body was transported for burial at sea.

No one will deny that it was one of the greatest love affairs in history. The letters between Edwina and Nehru were always referred to as The Love Letters. Mountbatten told Marie Seton, 'letters from him to me were always typed but letters to Edwina were always handwritten.' Her younger sister Mary said, 'Edwina had no will where he was concerned.'

A SPIRITUAL BOND: EDWINA AND NEHRU | 59

The love between Edwina and Nehru was born out of their joint anxiety and concern for India before and after the transfer of power. Its depth and strength was witnessed by many who saw them together. Delhi, its broad Lutyens' avenues, its beautiful gardens, the cool marble corridors and low windowed rooms of Nehru's house, the state rooms, drawing rooms and bedrooms – slow turning ceiling fans, silent swinging *pankhas* of the residence – this was the setting of their growing friendship apart from a few precious days in the cool of Mashobra.

1948

8

My Marriages . . . The *Reet*

It was the year 1950. I was seven years old at that time, or I may be eight or nine years old, because no one told me about my exact year of birth. To be honest, I never asked, it was not significant.

But I vaguely remember that I was playing in the courtyard, when three-four people, all men, came to our house. I was a little surprised by the hustle bustle in the kitchen, my two aunts a few years elder to me, left me alone in the yard and went to the kitchen. For a few moments I continued to play alone but then I got bored.

As I entered the kitchen which was on the other side of the house, I sensed something crucial was happening. There was a jovial atmosphere in the room. My aunts were giggling, my mother was beaming (she hardly used to do that, she was a quiet and serious person) and my grandmother was kind of hopping here and there, full of energy and vitality.

Though I was very young but I had a premonition that all this was related to me.

I felt scared but no one took notice of me, they were preparing something on the *chullah*, I don't exactly remember what it was. My aunts were talking to each other in whispers and occasionally stared at me, this frightened me more and I started crying and ran out of the kitchen into the fields.

I do not know when those people went away but they spoilt my peace of mind. After a few days I forgot the incident. A few years later another group of men came. It was similar to the earlier visit but it was more elaborate and more pronounced, or maybe I had grown older. I must be ten by now.

You see, in our small village everyone knew everyone else so when strangers came to your house the occasion demanded some interest. I don't remember whether they were the same people who had come earlier or not, I was still a child. But unlike the previous time when everyone had ignored me, this time my grandmother and my aunts were pouring their affection on me. Each one of them kissed my little head several times. I think I was never loved so lovingly till then. Even my youngest aunt, Ganga, kissed me on the head. I remembered how she hated my lice-filled head!

Except for my father who looked a little sad everyone seemed happy. He alone was frowning. His words to the ladies of the house dug deep into my small beating heart, 'Get her ready in ten minutes, they have to leave.'

Now, I was definitely scared, I started crying. Where was he sending me? And why? I hated my father, I thought he loved me dearly. He looked at me as I cried, just shook his head and went away.

On top of that my mother was nowhere to be seen (I didn't know that she was in labour and was giving birth to my brother in a small thatched roof cow-shed. I was told later that when I had stepped out of our village my first brother was born.) I felt miserable.

I don't remember even changing my clothes, my aunts and grandmother thrust a *potli* of clothes in my lap. It contained the two good suits that I possessed and one shawl (it was of my mother which they never allowed me to touch with admonition that *'it would get spoilt, it was not for children to touch'*).

My head was covered with a colourful *dhatu* which I had never worn earlier, and kind of pushed out of the room into the courtyard where those strangers stood waiting for me. I was not angry but more perplexed. 'Who were these people and why was I being sent with them, did I do anything wrong, did my father know that I had stolen *siddus* from the kitchen two days back or was he angry that I had torn the *salwar* of my new green suit while I was running in the field in a joyful mood pursued by my aunts.

I did not stop sobbing even when my father put his hand on my head and gave me a little push towards the waiting strangers. One of the men took my *potli* from me and the elderly one smiled at me (he was of my grandfather's age, but now I realise that he must not have been more than forty). One other thing that I remembered distinctly while leaving my house were my mother's screams, they were so alarming and frightening (I had no idea that she was giving birth and I also had no idea that it was so painful) that for a moment in between my crying I felt my heart stopped beating. Again, my child's mind concluded that I had done something very bad and that is why I was being punished along with my mother.

A little later when we had crossed our village, I stopped crying, as the strangers were good to me and the elderly one was the best, telling me not to worry, where we were going was my home only and I can play there to my heart's content and eat whatever I liked. The farther we went fear gave way to curiosity. I think I must have walked some three or four hours when we reached a small hamlet. There were a dozen or so people standing at the entrance and most of them were smiling which was a balm to my already exhausted and tired mind. There were two musicians who were playing *shehnai* and group of old ladies were singing a song which I did not understand.

My tiredness gave way to elation as I felt a little important, they were all patting and hugging me. I don't remember with whom I slept but the meal for which a lot of people (more than fifty) had been invited was delicious.

In the morning my mood swung again, I felt alienated when I saw everything new around me, I started crying. And I didn't stop till the strangers promised me that they will take me back to my house after a few days.

Now, when I look back, I feel I was so silly, but at that time I didn't know I had been married!

Then my elation to see my father and a couple of people from my village the next day! They had brought *sattu*, walnuts and apples besides other eatables, there was a lot of hustle bustle in the stranger's house. I ran to my father and told him that I wanted to go back to my amma, and started crying with all my might. The ladies in the house tried to pull me from my father's legs which I had clutched not letting go.

I felt my father softening and the more I knew he was softening the more my wailing became louder. In the end I succeeded in my mission. When I was leaving clutching the *potli* hard to my little bosom scared that they will take it away from me, I heard one of the ladies say, 'she must be the bride who stayed the least in the in-laws' house.' I realised that I had been married! But at that age it was not at all important to me, I was missing my house and wanted to go back. As I skipped back happy and carefree my father's mood also brightened up and when I saw my village, I was so excited that I left him behind and ran to my house. I realised how much I loved my grandmother, aunts and mother whom I had always taken for granted. I felt as if many years had gone by since I had left them though it was the first and only day of my life when I had remained away from my house and family. This was very significant to my small mind.

My aunts and grandmother were quite shocked and perplexed to see me and they frowned their displeasure. But

I didn't mind, my happiness had no bounds. I was back in the security of my family. I got to know that my mother was still in the cow-shed, I ran there to find a small baby, my brother, and my exhausted mother who was more shocked than happy to see me. I didn't mind anything now, I had a real toy to play with.

In the next few years two more brothers came into the world. And with the birth of my brothers, the villagers said, my father's fortunes changed, earlier he was an average farmer, now his orchard was producing very fine apples which were being sent all over India. And with this apple revolution our economic status changed, we became one of the richest few in the Kotgarh area.

My second marriage took place after three years. This time I had an idea of what marriage was about and was quite scared when a group of people came for the betrothing ceremony. One month later they came again, this time to take me along with them.

This time I did not cry nor felt guilty that I had done something wrong but I was definitely sad. My mother bade me farewell with my two small brothers tied on her back. I understood that there was no way out and I had to follow the strangers who had been treated lavishly with good food and wine by my father. One of the men took the 'potli' which was a little heavier with my bridal stuff. This time I had to walk 1½ hours only, it was the second time in my short life that I was leaving my village and it reminded me of that day three years back when there was a group, though different, of people waiting to welcome me. This time I was a little shy and tried to look out for my husband. It was the next day that the skinny, dark haired boy of about 14 years was pointed out to me as the *dulha*. My married life was little longer this time – one month. My husband left for his studies at Rampur the very next day. And I didn't see him after that. Life was very similar to one that I had left behind in my village except for the food. My new family was not very rich and my mother-in-law was expecting another child, my grand-*sasu* was not well and bed-ridden, I didn't mind the work that I had to do in these circumstances but it was lack of variety in food.

All the tasty dishes-meat, *patande*, *askalis* – if there were any had to be given to the men and the two ladies, I was always left with *sukhi roti* of maize and purified butter (which was in abundance in every household, as all kept cattle). For nearly a month I ate this boring diet which not only was bad in nutrition but was stale. This made me angry and frustrated. So, one day when my *saas* scolded me for something that I had done wrong (which I had) I made up my mind to leave the house. On one pretext or the other I found excuses to go to my village and landed to the surprise of my parents at home escorted by a few village women. I never went back and told my father that I did not like the food there. There was a lot of amusement in the house on my return.

My father asked the *gur* (medium of deity through whom the god speaks when questioned) of local *devta* about my fate. The *gur* told him that he should allow me to do what

I wanted and that something good will happen ultimately.

Then after four years, my third marriage took place. It was more explicit. This time a huge procession had come, by now the custom of plains that a *baraat* should go to the girl's house had entered the hills. My *sasural* was in a big village, day's walk away. I was fully conscious and a little excited to become a bride again. I was being chided all around by the women, 'not to come back again.' I had got to know a few months back that in both my earlier marriages father had to pay 'reet' to my in-laws.

Reet was an amount that was paid by to the husband of a lady if she decided to marry someone else or return to her parents' house. It was normal in those days for a lady to leave her husband if she got interested in someone else. In all such cases the next husband compensated the earlier one. In my case my father gave this customary money.

'Now he is a rich man, he won't mind giving *reet*,' I cheekily replied to the uproar of women. He was now the richest man in the village and I was going into one of the richest families as a bride.

My father gave a big feast where both vegetarian and non-vegetarian dishes were cooked. Entire village was invited and this time I had a trunk of clothes to take with me.

For the whole of next day, the marriage party accompanied with musicians, walked. They stopped many times on the way to dance and be merry. The marriage party stayed the night on the way at my *mami's* place where my would-be bridegroom had come to take a look at me. I was quite offended and in despair when I realised that he was an old man. He must be about fifteen year elder to me, and to my young mind looked more like an uncle than a husband.

By this time I was mature enough not to object but accept my fate. The real shock came when I reached his house and got to know that he already had a wife. As she could not bear a child the family had decided to marry him again. I was so angry this time with my family, particularly with my father. Later, I came to know that it was my grandfather who fixed the match. As he was the only son of the richest man, the landlord of the village, my grandfather thought that it was the best match. But I was not prepared for it and not ready to become a second wife.

However, with a laden heart and shattered dreams I participated in all the ceremonies. This was the late 1950s, girls could not say what they wanted or what they liked. They had to follow first their father's and then their husband's footsteps. The one year that I stayed in that house with that man was the most terrible for me. It was not that the elder wife was dominating or anything. It was like a fairy tale gone sour.

I felt I had become an old woman. I do not remember much of that miserable time. I did not even realise that my mental anguish had made an impact on my physical condition.

When my younger brothers (I had four brothers by now) and my mother came to visit me, they could not conceal their shock and distress. My in-laws also complained that I was unlike other village girls, always remained inside the house and kept to myself. Moreover, one year had passed and I had not conceived. They showed their displeasure on this.

My mother requested them to send me with them for a few days and promised my in-laws that they will explain things to me. I had a burning anger that time in my heart, 'will they marry him a third time for a child? Let them do it, I don't care a bit.' Later, I realised that my mental anguish hindered my getting pregnant.

This time, however, everyone in my family was supportive. That man came two or three times to take me, but my family did not send me back on one pretext or the other. After staying with my parents for nearly one year away from that man and bleak atmosphere I had gained weight and became my earlier self. I started looking at life more positively though whenever alone a dread always used to be there of going back to that house and that person.

And then came Bhagsu Mate of PWD to our village. He was just two years elder to me, belonged to adjoining village and for him 'I was love at first sight' but for me it was gradual.

Our courtship lasted for six months before we plunged into matrimony. I used to go to collect grass for the cattle, and everyday our eyes met and talked in the common language of love. Later, we started to speak to each other. Though we were poles apart but our love was true. He was poor, I was rich, I was three times married, he was a bachelor.

There was a lot of opposition from our families. I did not want to elope, Bhagsu did not want to elope, I told my grandmother this and my desire to marry him. Once I even threatened to kill myself – how very stupid I was. It was do or die for me. My father was the first to agree though reluctantly. And I thank him from all my heart, it was a small ceremony but this time it was a *pakki* marriage (with religious rituals and *pheras*). Oh, so glad I am that I fought with everyone and took the decision to marry him.

I have been married now for 50 years.

Supported and encouraged by my father, Bhagsu left the job and became a contractor and we became rich. At last, I had my own fairy tale.

So, in the end my fourth marriage was for love but yes, this time it was my Bhagsu who gave the '*reet*' and not my father. Thank God, he only had one daughter.

1950s

9

Love In Simla

The movie *Love in Simla*, released in 1960, which introduced Sadhana Shivdasani and Joy Mukherjee to Hindi Cinema was an instant hit. Sadhana stole the heart of cine-goers.

But the real Love in Simla was between Sadhana and R.K. Nayyar, the director of the movie. Simla bewitched the sixteen-year-old Sadhana and twenty-two-year-old Nayyar and they fell in love.

Joy Mukherjee, the hero of the film remembers, 'Simla was really beautiful. I feel nostalgic even now after nearly fifty years. Our unit came here thrice for shooting. Film magazines started to write about the romance between Sadhana and Nayyar when we were in Simla. So, when we went back they were the hot topic of discussion at Bombay parties. As the movie was being filmed we, the main cast and the producer, director, would go to parties together, and this fuelled more gossip about them and everyone started to talk about their affair. Yes, the real Love in Simla was between Sadhana and R.K. Nayyar.'

It was on these romantic curving roads that the real lovers walked. Though they were together every minute of the shooting, they wanted to take time out alone which was difficult. As they covered different locales for shooting, these places – the Mall, Ridge, Peterhof gave them memories of a lifetime.

Sadhana, the only child of the Shivdasanis, a Sindhi family, was born in Karachi and was named after her father's favourite actress, Sadhana Bose. Her mother schooled her at home until she turned eight. They came to Mumbai at the time of Partition in 1947. She was fifteen years old when the film industry discovered her. Earlier, she had acted as a chorus girl in Raj Kapoor's Shree 420 in 1955.

What brought her attention was her second lead in a Sindhi film called *Abana* (1958) where she played the heroine's younger sister. She got admitted in an acting school run by film producer Sashadhar Mukherjee, which was training another aspiring actress, Asha Parekh. During the casting of *Dil Deke Dekho* (1959) Mukherjee asked the director Nasir Hussain to choose between Sadhana and Asha to play the heroine; Hussain chose Asha.

For his next project, *Love in Simla* (1960), Mukherjee again gave his director, R.K. Nayyar (Raj Kapoor's assistant) a choice for the heroine. Nayyar chose Sadhana, and she was paired with Mukherjee's own son, the new-comer Joy Mukherjee.

The film unit came to Simla and stayed at the Clarke's hotel on Mall Road. Nayyar and Sadhana liked to watch the shimmering lights of Simla town at night from the hotel. In the late 1950s, the Mall was very different from what it is today. It had a strong colonial hangover.

'It was always clean, spick and span and was washed regularly' recalls an octogenarian businessman of Shimla. 'All those people who came for a stroll here in the evenings were in formals, men dressed in suits with shining shoes and the ladies were invariably in saris. Rarely would one find people dressed in casuals and yes, there were no giggling, boisterous young girls and boys roaming here and there. The young men and women were well dressed, well behaved and children always accompanied the parents or other elders if at all they came to the Mall. It was nothing like this, the rude, mannerless crowd of today.' He adds, 'Oh yes, I saw Sadhana and Joy; Asha and many more . . . yes, Dimple was the fairest of them all . . . . People never hounded film stars, they kept a distance.'

Oh, the good old times . . . when the sky was blue and love was in the air . . . .

It is rumoured that Sadhana's parents threatened Nayyar in Simla with legal action if he did not end the relationship. They felt Sadhana was too young. She had a career to think about. Nayyar obliged and for some time kept his distance. But their love, pure and strong, did not die. It was also rumoured that her mother strongly disapproved of Nayyar. She often asked her daughter to marry 'someone like Rajinder Kumar.'

But in 1965, aided by her father Sadhana tied the knot with R.K. Nayyar.

Sadhana's films *Mere Mehboob* (1963), *Woh Kaun Thee* (1964), *Mera Saya* (1966), *Waqt* (1965), *Inteqam* (1969), *Ek Phool Do Mali* (1969) enthralled the audiences.

She decided to retire from acting after *Geeta Mera Naam* (1974) because she wanted her fans to remember her as a young, beautiful leading lady. With her husband, with whom she remained happily married for nearly thirty years till his death in the late nineties, she formed a production company.

Sadhana set fashion trends like the Sadhana Cut and the *churidar* which are still in vogue after five decades.

She keeps herself busy playing cards with friends at Mumbai's Otters Club, watching television and gardening. In keeping with her enigmatic image, she adamantly refuses to let herself be photographed in public.

Let us hear her story in her own words . . . .

'One day, in 1957–58 I think, a group of men had come to our college to pick out students to act in a Sindhi film based on the partition. The film was called Abana which means one's ancestral home. They saw one of my plays and selected me to play heroine as Shiela Ramani's younger sister. The film became a big hit. On the day of its release *Screen* had published a photograph of mine on its front page and Mr S. Mukherjee saw it and liked it. He had started his own company, Filmalaya, so he signed me for his first Hindi film *Love in Simla*. It was a first for everyone connected with the film – the banner, the Director R.K. Nayyar, the hero Joy Mukherjee, the heroine, me – we were all new. I was never the typical conventional beauty. The producer and the director wanted a cute, lively, innocent girl and they had decided that I suited the role. The concept of beauty in those days was based on the Audrey Hepburn look which was very much in vogue. Of course, conventional beauties like Meena Kumari and Madhubala were still considered gorgeous. Anyway, before I started to work on the film I underwent a training course at the Filmalaya acting school along with Joy.'

She recalls, 'Do you know how the famous Sadhana fringe originated? I have a broad forehead, so to make it narrow they tried to stick a strip near the hairline but it did not work. So, finally the director Nayyar took me to a beauty parlour at Kemps Corner and told the lady there to give me a Audrey Hepburn fringe. Little did we know at that time that this fringe would trigger off a new fashion wave. I became identified with my fringe, to the extent that people who did not know me couldn't recognise me without it! Even today, girls ask for the Sadhana fringe. I also started tight *churidar-kurta* and *mojris* look.'

On what Nayyar loved the most about her Sadhana recalled, 'R.K. Nayyar said he loved my nose, one could land a helicopter on it!' She added with characteristic candour, 'I was attractive but never beautiful. I am still essentially a very shy and private person. I don't socialise much but neither am I a recluse. I am a good housewife, my house runs on well oiled wheels. I have completed 26.5 years of marriage but the honeymoon is still on. I remember a couple of years ago, Nayyar and I had gone to a party and after the usual greetings we sat in a corner and soon we were busy talking, oblivious of anyone around when a lady came and introduced to us as Mrs Farookh Shaikh. She told us that she had been watching us for the last 45 minutes and that after so many years of marriage we had so much to say to each other and she told us that if after 24 years of marriage she could have so much to say to her husband she would consider herself lucky. I was so thrilled by her compliment.'

She said, 'I want my fans to remember me as the Sadhana of *Love in Simla* . . . .'

1960s

10

A Love Song That Changed Their Lives

One song – a song which is on everyone's lips, a song which is sung by all in diverse festivities, a tune to which both young and old sway, a song which is sung by many lovers to woo their beloveds.

A song which initiated trends of rhythmic beats in *pahari* music in the late 1970s, a song which became a cult of that era and still goes on – a song with a mysterious lyricist, a song whose story no one is familiar with.

This is a song which affected the lives of two individuals, a song which turned their lives topsy-turvy, a song which shattered their dreams, a song which is never sung in their presence. This is a song to whose melody they have never swayed and tapped their feet to its music and lyrics . . . *O ladi Shanta* . . . .

Yes, this is a love song based on them.

I received Shanta's letter yesterday. She gave me the permission to go ahead and write her story. This is a story that she has never told anyone, a story that no one asks her about and the few who did she did not have the guts to relate. This is a story which is very popular, a story which is misinterpreted and exaggerated in everyone's mind. A story which changed the course of her life.

This story she related to me with tears brimming in her beautiful eyes and the intense pain of unfulfilled dreams and desires. This is a story which still haunts and torments her as her son grows up and demands that the song be banned. This is a story whose truth and accuracy no one knows.

Nearly three decades back, Shanta was a fifteen-year-old studying in Government School at Matiana, forty-five kilometres from Shimla, a small village on the Hindustan Tibet road (The lyrics are wrong in saying that she studied in Portmore). Hailing from an illustrious family of sports people, she topped in sports in her school. From sixth standard onwards she played not only for State championships but also the Nationals. She was one of the best players that Himachal ever had in volleyball. Fair, beautiful and tall, Shanta had no worries in life and was busy making a career for herself in sports. She was at par with known sportspersons of Himachal including Suman Rawat.

She was engaged when she was born. Later, the boy was a student in the same school with her.

When she was in the eighth standard she befriended Basant who was a student of Government College at Shimla.

He too belonged to Matiana. The boundaries of their land joined and Shanta had to cross his house while going to school.

Basant was engaged to a girl in a nearby village. In fact, all his four brothers were engaged to four sisters in the same family. He was the youngest and the only one left to be married. When Basant returned from Shimla they talked to each other occasionally while she was going to school or coming back.

Theirs was an innocent friendship – a platonic relationship. Shanta who used to travel outside her village for different sports events and meet people from diverse areas had no problem conversing with boys and thus got along well with Basant, too. Their fleeting meetings gradually grew into something stronger than friendship but that was all. Marriage at that time was not a priority.

Both of them wanted to build their careers. They were bright and had the talent to excel in their respective domains. Shanta got a scholarship in sports from Punjab University. She was only seventeen-years-old when her life crumbled like a pack of cards.

'Won't it be right to grieve when life offers you a dream so far from any of your expectations, and you are unable to accept it? I was just a simple girl from a far-off village and was being offered a scholarship to study further.' she asked of me. I had no answer. 'Oh, how can I forget that day? I had just finished knitting a sweater for myself (we call it *koti*), baby pink in colour with delicate shiny buttons. I had to try it on and was trying to put it off till father came from Shimla. His was the only room where there was a decent mirror to look at. It was not full size but at least bigger than the bathroom mirror that we had in the balcony. I was eager to see myself in that *koti*. I had especially worn my favourite suit, white in colour with pink dots to match.

The radio was tuned to Shimla station. Radio was more than just a technology-driven tool, it was an indispensable part of our lives. We were all addicted to and obsessed with it. Radio Ceylon, the Urdu service of All India Radio and Shimla station had enthralled us. I was passionate about *pahari* songs, and regional language programmes and *dhara-re-geet* were our favourites. At that time *pahari natis* were echoing in the house. I loved the soul searching, melodious voice of Himachali singers.'

'Father was expected any time. The voice on the radio announced that a new nati . . . O, lari Shanta would be sung by Mr Lachi Ram Bhardwaj. It was like listening to any other programme, I least expected such a big catastrophe to fall on me. The title 'Shanta' too did not ring a bell. It was a common name. Never in my wildest dreams could I have thought that it was referring to me. It was like slow-poison, there was nothing instant about the shock. It kind of seeped slowly into the blood. The words . . . *Shanta, Santu, Jhalru de nalle, volleyball* all floated in mid-air and only when it ended did I realise that the song was a distorted version of my life. It took a few moments for my family members to put two and two together. They had no inkling that I was on talking terms with Santu (Basant's nickname) . . . and ever since that ill-fated day I forgot what it meant to be young and free.

My father came late, his eyes piercingly angry. A chill ran down my spine. He looked away and went to his room, closing the door with a bang. This really scared me. I never tried on that sweater. It had lost its charm for me.

A part of me wanted to go to Shimla and confront this Bhardwaj and All India Radio and demand to know how they could make such a false and shameless song on me. For nights I remained sleepless, tossing and turning in bed – imagining what I would say and how I would fight with them. But, I was too young and did not have the guts to do it. I used to be such a trusting person but now no more. Thereafter, we stopped listening to the radio in our house.

Henceforth, seconds, minutes, hours seemed to drag on. It seemed as if my life had come to a standstill. For hours I would sit on my balcony staring blankly at nothing in particular. I had no one to unload my misery on or tell my side of the story to. I was a laughing stock, a topic for gossip, a characterless girl. My near-and-dear ones gave me the cold shoulder, too. I realised I was responsible for ruining my family's name and my own reputation. I began to feel the world was talking about me.

Her engagement was broken and so was Basant's.

Cultural norms were so different then, there was no friendship between boys and girls, just affairs. Love marriages were rare and taboo. If couples fell in love it was all hushed up and converted into arranged marriage. If a boy and girl talked in the open the girl was labelled a 'loose' character.

'It was not so bad for me', said Basant, 'though people sniggered and laughed and talked behind my back. But I was not tortured like she was. Being a boy I was saved from the hell and suffering that Shanta had to go through. I too heard the song on radio. There were no telephones then and we did not write letters. I was worried to death about what she would be facing. I could not meet her when I reached Matiana after a few days. Whenever I heard someone sing this song I turned livid and once fought with some boys, but it was of no use. The song was on everybody's lips'.

They had to go through a harrowing experience. She gave up sports because wherever she went, people talked about her and the song in hushed tones. The lyrics in the song were not true – they had never met secretly, they had always met in the open and their relationship was pure and clean unlike what the song suggested.

They also never went to *Jhalru de nalle* and she never studied at Portmore School. She was grounded both by her family and her own unwillingness to face people's stares. She had to make a decision, she had no choice, she had to let go of her ambition and get married to Basant.

Basant's family approached her family and the elders decided that under the circumstances this was the best course of action.

ೞ

'Shanta, thirty years have passed, do you regret this relationship?'

'No, never. I loved him then, I still love him but yes the song, it hurt me.'

'It is now a part of the folklore, we will die one day but this song will be sung by many and our love will always be remembered,' Basant said smiling gently.

They looked at each other, the love between them alive and tangible. Holding hands they declared that in the end love is more important than ambitions. Thankfully, a loving heart can withstand and survive emotional storms. And life is worth living when you know that the one you love did not fail you when you were in distress.

'Not many women have had their love put to such a hard test. I am fortunate that my husband is so supportive. What else do I need!' proclaimed Shanta.

1970s

11

Forever Twenty

This is a story which has no ending. Even now, the very thought of that two-year courtship brightens my day and I am twenty again! It is as if those moments that we shared together never passed, they just melted in the treasure trove of my heart and became pearls. These pearls are with me forever.

It was the year 1989.

Even as I speak I can feel her fragrance about me and my whole body tingles with that peculiar feeling when you are in love for the first time. The sensation and awareness that we belonged to each other has never left me. Our bond is the deepest and it is beyond mere physical fascination. We know each other's thoughts and feelings without having to speak about them and that can only happen when you love with a pure and innocent heart.

I have a wife and two children whom I love dearly. I would not have things any other way and I am absolutely happy. It is very hard for people to comprehend this.

Even if I am given a wish to alter my past, I would not like to do so. I prefer it to happen just the way it happened. I do not want to lose that uncertainty, that longing. This is something which I can never explain in mere words. The concept of time does not hold for us. It will always be the same whether we meet after ten or fifteen or twenty years. She will smile and I will smile back. Our world will become brighter and it will be as if we were twenty again.

☙

Rocky and Seema. One a very good friend of mine and the other just an aquaintance. These two lovebirds were neighbours in Annadale. Rocky was the happy-go-lucky variety while Seema was practical, mature, reserved. Seema's family consisted of a younger brother studying in Class Seven, a working mother and an overbearing, wife-beating alcoholic father. Seema was always in dread of her father and believed that if any of them defied him he would not only punish, he could even kill their mother.

When the father is not in the house the ambience changes but when he is around all the curtains are drawn, everyone talks in whispers. Seema does not laugh, dresses shabbily, is like a dead doll.

Her mother finds it impossible to confront her husband. She bears everything in silence. She emotionally blackmails her children to be docile and submissive. There is a perpetual air of fear in that house.

The atmosphere in Rocky's house is quite different. They are four brothers, his mother is a housewife and his father, a senior engineer. The father is usually in and out of depression, yet the family as a whole remains cheerful.

Rocky's father has put in thirty years of hard work in a government job but his life became hell as he was an honest man. He would not take bribes and commissions. His colleagues thought he was out of place and insane. He also tried to challenge the corrupt – both within and outside the department. This led to frequent transfers, explanations and harassment at the workplace. He went into regular bouts of depression, remained mostly on medical leave or leave without pay. Thus, the financial position of Rocky's family was quite bad, but it was the *never say die* spirit of the family, their sense of humour and wit that made them survive against odds.

Both families lived in rented accommodation on the ground floor in adjoining buildings. The courtyard was common.

Rocky was liked by all in the neighbourhood. He was helpful, witty, made everyone laugh and had that 'no threat' aura around him which made parents of young girls safe – 'he is not that kind of boy' they told themselves. So, he could be commonly seen on the roofs of houses in the locality, adjusting their TV antennas or otherwise changing their gas cylinders or helping mothers and daughters carry huge *martbaans* of pickle.

Rocky's family had been living in Annadale for many years when Seema's parents moved there. As expected, Seema's mother liked the boy and Rocky became friends with Seema and her younger brother. Both were in their early twenties and studied at the Himachal Pradesh University. Gradually, their friendship blossomed.

He felt good, warm and secure with her and she reciprocated the feelings. He started coming to their house on one pretext or the other, always in the absence of her father. And this proximity grew into love.

ଔ

It was Seema who made the first physical advance and the only one in our two-year courtship. I had gone to their house to hand over medicine for her younger brother who was suffering from flu. It had now become a routine for me to visit them when the parents were not there. For hours we would talk and laugh about anything and everything under the sun.

As I handed the medicine to Seema she caught hold of my hand and to my astonishment kissed my palm. This was my first kiss, all warm and tickly. I was both delighted and embarrassed at the same time. I did not wash the hand she kissed for more than ten days. In wonder I would stare at it and kiss it passionately a number of times a day. I had never been in love with this hand as I was then.

From that day onwards our romance started and with time it flourished. Apart from seeing each other at home we began to meet secretly.

We met at Shahji's and enjoyed tea and *besan barfi*. Invariably we had our lunch at Calm Café – *rajmah-chawal* or *aloo paranthas* dripping with butter. Many times in the evenings we would walk from Summer Hill to Boileauganj through the forest path below the Indian Institute of Advanced Study to eat *doodh-jalebi* at Krishna Sweet Shop.

෴

All of us who knew them felt that nothing would come out of this romance. Her parents would never agree to their marriage. Not only was he unemployed, their castes were different. It was amusing to see them trying to keep their love secret because all the neighbours knew about it. It was so apparent.

As her father left at 9.15 in the morning, both came out in the courtyard to chat. They were not seen outside after her father returned at 6 in the evening.

When they went to the University, they followed a pattern. He left a few minutes earlier than her and stood near the entrance to the Annadale ground from where they walked up the footpath that climbed through thick Deodar forest. When they came back from University she reached five minutes earlier than him. They were so engrossed in themselves and confident of their secret that the comments passed by the people in the neighbourhood did not register:

'Are you going alone to the university today?' 'Aur aaj kahan ghoom kar aaye ho?' but they were in love and answered these questions in full seriousness to the amusement of the *mohalla*-crowd.

☙

Hitler – as I called her father – nearly discovered us one day. He was such a stickler for punctuality that it was possible to predict his actions to the minute. He was also a strict rule-maker. He would draw the curtains whenever he left the house and check these again when he returned to see if there was any change. In all those years that we lived as neighbours he left at 9.15 am sharp and returned at 6 pm sharp. But one day we 'escaped murder'.

On that fateful day he returned home in the afternoon. She, her younger brother and I were watching the movie *Ijazat* on a hired VCR when suddenly Seema saw her father from a window, climbing the stairs. She jumped up, her face pale and in a hoarse whisper just said, 'Papa.'

Both of us jumped, too. My heartbeat intensified and I felt I was facing a death squad. For a few seconds we all stood numb in shock not knowing what to do. Then, we heard his footsteps outside the main door. Everything happened simultaneously. She went to open the door for her father, I ran to go into hiding in the bathroom, her brother yanked the VCR cable from the socket and concealed it under the bed. The bathroom opened out to a small lobby that led to the main entrance of the house and this was the only door from which I could leave. I was dead. I cursed myself for putting her in trouble.

To say that nothing happened that day would be absurd.

My legs were shaking, my heart pounding. What if he opened the bathroom door? My fingers were trembling and I could not even shut the door properly, leave alone bolt it from the inside.

Then the impossible happened. I heard my love say, 'Papa, *main ek minute baahar se towel utha leti hoon*' (just a minute, I will bring the towel from outside). I opened the door, not knowing where Hitler was. I saw his back towards me, he was grumbling something about the open curtains. Her brother's face was towards me and he was looking at me, his mouth open. I slipped out as Seema entered with the towel. Our eyes met for a second and then I heard the door close behind me. He could have turned any moment and seen me. I shivered with dread as I ran from the house. My legs had turned to jelly. I was surprised that he had not guessed something was amiss from the shocked faces of his son and daughter. But maybe, they were always like that when he was around.

೧೩

Then a catastrophe occured. Seema's father found a match for her.

All friends got together in the Rose Garden of the Indian Institute of Advanced Study. We advised them to elope. As Rocky was jobless we offered to support them with our meagre pocket money. Other wild schemes were considered. But Seema was adamant. If eloped, her father would kill her mother and even her brother. No, she had to do whatever he said. The boy came to see Seema, we invented all sorts of schemes to drive him away but all in vain. The *rishta* was finalised and the marriage fixed. He was a NRI working in Singapore.

ଔ

She convinced me it was over for us. For days we talked on the phone. Oh, how we used to talk! There was just a landline then. I used to call her up at night when everyone had gone to sleep hidden under the *rajai* with the phone, talking in a muffled voice. When I heard any noise – someone coughing or anyone turning in the bed – I would put the phone down abruptly and act as if I had been snoring. In whispers we talked about our impossible future. Sometimes we didn't speak but just cried, listening to each other.

Our telephone bill soared.

It was my first and sweetest love, and my heart still beats and yearns for those days spent together. The excitement and the thrill of being able to keep the affair secret and the constant danger of being caught by Hitler or sniffing neighbours was the spice of our life.

ଔ

Then he hit upon a brilliant idea.

Let her go now. She can come back after a few months of her marriage. Her father will have no say then.

We could not understand how this could happen. We believed in the 'once married, always married' theory. Rocky was at least a decade ahead of Bollywood and its blockbusters like *Dhadkan* and *Hum Dil De Chuke Sanam*. He was really in love and quite capable of accepting Seema in his life after one year of marriage. The trend was changing and we were becoming the old generation. He had to talk to Seema about the idea and convince her.

ଓ

Deeply imprinted in my memory are the days when I followed Seema and the other guy (who was to be her husband) wherever they went in Shimla after their engagement. It was then that I realised the intensity of my love. My heart cried when I saw them at places where we had gone together: the temples – Jakhu, Sankat Mochan and Tara Devi; tourist spots – Kufri, Chail and of course, the Indian Institute of Advanced Study which had been our main rendezvous.

Ignoring the voice of reason I decided on a strategy. It was sheer madness. My world had come to an end when I realised that she was drifting away from me. I felt the agony of love.

I told Seema about my plan, 'Don't feel bad about it. If that is how it must be, I will wait. I will find a job and before one year has ended. You come back to me, leave him. It is not our final goodbye.'

I said this, believing with all my heart that she would return to me. Days passed and it was as if my heart was dead, my lips silent. My limbs were the only thing that were alive.

People asked me if I was ill. I was just twenty then and though one cannot believe at that time young hearts seldom stay broken.

ೞ

She got married and flew to Singapore. She called him up frequently. We too received her calls. With each call his mood swung from depression to exhilaration. It all depended on what she talked about.

He had a drink for the first time the day she got married. Many of us felt that she was making a fool of him. But no one had the guts to tell him this. What if we were wrong? What if she actually came?

ೞ

Weeks passed and we talked regularly on the phone about our future plans. But slowly 'he' started filtering into the conversations. She would tell me that he was not a bad guy, was tender and sensitive to her feelings. He was providing her with all the material comforts which I would not have been able to give her. As I slowly accepted him here in Shimla she accepted him there in Singapore. Our telephone calls became less frequent. Then after six months she was with child. It was an awful blow to me. And then time, the great healer, intervened and I let go.

But sometimes in a pensive mood I still see her laughing and chatting and my heart aches for a second, terribly missing those enchanted moments.

ଔ

Life goes on, and it did for him, too.

1989

12

Everlasting Love

'Hi,'

'Hi' said Ruchi, flicking the straight long hair away from her face. She was not beautiful, but so pretty that it hurt. Ruchi was his colleague in the telecom company at Kasumpti, Shimla. For twenty-eight-year-old Neeraj it was love at first sight.

She looked very young but as she was Customer Manager, she must be older, he calculated.

Today was a significant day for him. He had told his elder sister about her. Now, he had decided to go for it.

For the last two months he had been dropping hints to her about his feelings. But she always ignored or took these lightly. She was too casual towards him. He had to set his mind and heart at peace.

Six months of being involved and not being able to convey his feelings had been agony. Only a person in love could understand his state of mind. Now, he had to know her answer – yes or no.

When he saw her six months back on joining the Shimla office, he was instantly charmed by her. It was because of Ruchi that he had refused his transfer back to Delhi. He would come an hour early to the office and leave as late as possible. It was not that Ruchi stayed long hours in office, but that when she was there he could do no work. So, his work was done either in the morning before she came or in the evening after she left. He had been watching her for so many days now, he could decipher every emotion on her face.

'Here it is,' said Ruchi handing, him two folders. She had a clear white skin, deep dark eyes, a lovely kissable mouth. He yearned to hold her in his arms. His stomach contracted at the thought that she might not be interested in him. There would be scores of men after her. How could a MBA from a small town in Haryana compete with her great admirers.

'Boss, are you fine?' asked Ruchi anxiously. It was her style to call him 'boss' though he was her senior colleague.

'No, I am not fine, Ruchi. I was just wondering about you.'

'Me?' she said, boredom creeping into her voice.

'Yes, you.'

'What is it boss, I am busy,' she said.

'So am I.'

'What do you want?' She was rude now.

'Let us go out for lunch,' he said bravely.

'It is not lunch time.'

'So, for tea.'

'Is it important?' she said, her face now serious and concerned.

Important? It is my life, he thought, but said, 'yes,' taking her hand.

It was a spontaneous gesture for him and he was alarmed as she jerked her hand away.

'Okay.' She gave him an unsure smile. 'Is it regarding the job?'

'No.'

'Then I hope you are not wasting my time,' she said, rolling her eyes, trying to sound stern.

He touched her shoulder where her hair lay like a thick blanket and impulsively pushed a strand back. She jerked again. He shrugged. His boldness had increased. In the last five minutes he had touched her twice. He was surprised. For the last six months he had kept his distance from her.

In about ten minutes they were seated across each other at the Ashiana restaurant in Chota Shimla. It was the best restaurant near the office.

'Shoot,' she said mockingly.

Neeraj's confidence level was depleting fast. He did not know where to start, what to say or what to ask. He started off with the stupidest question, 'I hope you don't think this is too personal.' God damn it, it was personal, what could be more personal than this?

'No', she said, 'carry on.' As he racked his brain on what to say her mobile started ringing. She muttered a sorry and picked it up. He waited eagerly. It was her sister. She chatted enthusiastically, oblivious of his growing nervousness. The conversation ended and she looked at him and said, 'Okay, shoot.' She seemed to love the word shoot.

'First, you switch off your mobile,' he said.

'Oh, is it that important? Suppose I get a call from the office?'

'I will handle it.'

'Alright. Now shoot.'

Again the word shoot. Now he was definitely feeling low, his determination was ebbing.

'Tell me something about yourself,' he said lamely.

She raised her beautifully shaped eyebrows.

'I mean about your family and all,' he added.

'My family lives in Shimla, I have a sister in Delhi,' she said, a crooked smile playing on her angelic face.

'I know that,' he said exasperated both by his not being able to communicate and by her casual approach to his state of mind.

'Neeraj, I am a widow.'

'What!' he said, jumping from his seat, tilting the cup of coffee on the table.

'Calm down.'

'What?' he repeated stupidly.

'Yes, I am a widow. I lost Abhishek a year ago.'

'Oh.' And then he stammered, 'I . . . I . . . didn't know.'

'How long were you married?' he said after a few moments of silence, his heart beating hard against his ribs.

'Fourteen years.'

'What?'

'Yes, I am forty.'

'You look . . . ' he was shaken. He struggled to accept what she was saying.

'Is there anything else you want to know?' she asked softly.

He opened his mouth to speak but no words came out.

'I'll catch up with you at office,' she said, getting up.

Speechless, he stared at her, at the pain in her eyes as she walked out and into the bright sunshine of December.

ଔ

Her affair with Abhishek began in the year 1990. She had been crowned Miss English and he was enthroned as Mr MBA in the Himachal Pradesh University. Their free display of love, confidence level and attitude were the envy of both boys and girls.

They were the most talked about couple in the campus as they were not secretive like others. Abhishek would zoom past on his bike with Ruchi clinging to him. This fired the imagination of an entire generation of students. Boys longed to own a bike which was not easy back then, while girls dreamed of being with someone who owned a bike, someone stylish and rich like Abhishek.

She remembered those romance-filled days. They were young and in love. Every day was full of newness and beauty. Moreover, they were in the most romantic of places – Shimla. What else could one ask for!

They fell for each other during the rehearsal of a cultural function in the university auditorium. The academic session had just commenced and the campus was buzzing with activities. The lawns of the Indian Institute of Advanced Studies were full of students and ragging sessions were on. Student wings of political parties – SFI, NSUI, ABVP – were warming up to elections so there were frequent disruptions to classes.

In this atmosphere his bike was a great liberating force. Every day they went to nearby places: Kamna Devi, Annadale, Glen, Chadwik Fall, Kiarighat, Naldehra, Cregneno, Mashobra, Wild Flower Hall, Kufri and Chail. They could be seen lost in each other in a corner in the favourite eating joints in and around town: University Café, Baljees, Aunties, Pappis and Embassy.

They walked hand-in-hand on the railway track from Summer Hill to the Shimla railway station and crossed long tunnels which was scary and romantic at the same time – walking so close to each other on the narrow gauge rail track surrounded by thick rhododendron, pine and oak trees.

The scare, thrill, excitement and the romance of it all came back to Ruchi. The Summer Hill–Shimla and Summer Hill–Jutogh section of the railway track is witness to so many blossoming romances. It is the repository of so many love stories, tales of young love and romance . . . if only it could speak . . . .

Their favourite temple was Kamna Devi, located on a small hill-top near Boileauganj. There were three idols inside the small shrine. Mahakali on the left, Lakshmi in the centre and Saraswati on the right.

A small tree stood at the entrance of the temple. People came to tie bright red *dories* around its branches whenever wished for something. It was a wishing tree. Ruchi too had tied a piece of her *dupatta* praying for their life together. The story of the temple fascinated her. The place was earlier known as Kreera Devi, the playground of the goddess. When the Viceregal Lodge was to be built in Simla in nineteenth century, the Commander in Chief of the British Army in India said that he wanted his house to be built on an equally high spur. So Kamna Hill, then called Prospect Hill was selected. But there was the problem of shifting the temple. The British did not believe in local tradition that the temple should not be shifted. But when they started construction wherever they dug honey bees swarmed out of the ground and they had to abandon the project.

Potters Hill was another favourite haunt of young lovers but there was a problem. Whenever they walked towards Potters Hill, they had to go past the boy's hostel and if any hosteller was around and saw them he would call the others to shout and boo. But that had its own thrill.

More than anything else, walks on the forest road, the Lovers Lane as it was called then, were the high point. It was then she realised how romantic the walks in Shimla were. On Sundays and other outing days, they would start at the Navbahar Chowk and went past Machhi Wali Kothi to the Christ Church. At other times, they strolled on the upper forest road and then climbed down to the Ridge from the Titla Hotel side after passing through the Five Benches.

The walk took them about four hours . . . but four hours full of romance.

The sunshine came through the trees and made strange patterns on the road. Whenever they sat for rest, these patterns were formed on her dress and face. He studied these patterns and recited verses from Urdu poets which made her heart sing. Ruchi sang his favourite songs.

They were probably the only couple who openly showed their affection without any guilt, fear or shame. As a result, Abhishek was branded a *fukra*, a rich boy exhibiting his richness through his bike and branded clothes and she was a *fast* girl openly going out with him.

She had put up a collage of their photographs on a wall of her room in the hostel and other girls used to enter her room on one pretext or the other just to *see* it with their own eyes.

Their relationship started another trend. Abhishek's sister Arti not only knew about the affair, she sat with them at the University Café and at Shahjis. It was unknown at that time for the would-be-*bhabhi* to openly share this kind of friendship with her would-be-*nanad*.

There were many who said: 'This is a wrong recipe for marriage, Ruchi will loose, he will not marry her. I am ready to give in writing, it will not mature, let us have a bet, when it comes to marriage boys prefer a simple girl,' etc . . . etc . . .

All lost the bet when they got married on 12 May 1992. They spent fourteen glorious years together before tragedy struck.

It was the day after their marriage that Abhishek was diagnosed with a chronic illness. Despite all precautions that they took he succumbed to the disease. They had gone to Delhi for his treatment but there he became desperately ill. He was in the ICU. It was so difficult to watch him struggle for life.

She stood outside the ICU glass wall that separated them, tears streaming down her face as he opened his eyes for the last time, conveying his love. In agony Ruchi watched him take his last breath – and so ended their love story.

☙

Life did not end for Ruchi. A year later her heart still yearned for those days they spent together but she told herself she would not be fair to the loving bond they shared by being unhappy. Both of them had lived by the dictum 'we live only once'. This was what had made them express their love so openly in the University days. And after his death she had to continue living life to the full.

1990

13

The Sanyasi

'Swami*ji*, we have no other option. We have to go to the district administration.'

Swami Ramanand looked at his disciple and nodded his head. He was clad in the saffron robes of the ashram. His disciple was in white clothes as he was still learning. Swami Ramanand was well-built and fair-complexioned with deep-set eyes. Years of solitude, reading of scriptures and long hours of devotional singing and daily meditation had given calmness and peace to him which reflected on his face. He had a kind and loving face, he was always smiling.

The disciple was right. They had to go to the district administration. The matter could not be resolved with dialogue any more. They had been trying to negotiate and come to a compromise for more than three years but all in vain.

Swami Ramanand hated going to government offices. In fact, he detested venturing out of his Kasauli Ashram.

Sometimes, he wondered at the irony of his having to deal with worldly affairs even after becoming a sanyasi.

The more senior he grew in his organisation the more he got involved in the management of the ashram. So many times he felt the urge to tell his Guruji that the purpose and intention of his joining the ashram and becoming a sanyasi was to leave behind all worldly affairs and responsibilities but this was hardly happening. Whenever he was discharging the administrative and managerial duties in the ashram, the guilty conscience of leaving his younger brothers and sisters without any help gnawed at him.

When he came out of the four walls of the ashram this guilt became more pronounced and it was becoming unbearable now. He had been carrying this regret for the last fifteen years and every time he did any odd job in and out of the ashram that was 'worldly' his wounds re-opened and became fresh.

Fifteen years ago he had shed his responsibility as the 'eldest' in the family. The pain of leaving behind three sisters, all younger to him, without any plan for their future always pricked his conscience. Their parents died in an accident when he was a second year student of Hotel Management in Calcutta. He had to leave in between to take care of the family business and also to look after his siblings.

'So, when should we go?' his disciple interrupted his reverie.

Well if we have to go, we must go early. Today, in fact just now, or the DC will not get to know the real story, he thought.

'It is better if we finish the matter off early rather than linger.' His disciple read his thoughts.

'Let us go then,' Swami Ramanand said getting up.

They came out of the ashram and walked towards the car. Though his Guru ji had several ashrams in hill stations – Mussorie, Dagshai, Nainital – Swami Ramanand liked Kasauli the best. He had requested his Guru ji to allow him to look after the Kasauli ashram. It was not only a small, quiet hill-station but also the summer home of Khushwant Singh – his favourite author when he was in college. Swami Ramanand thought many times that Khushwant Singh would have denounced his renunciation as a big fraud. This idea always amused him and also pained him.

Kasauli was also the place where the anti-rabies vaccine had been developed by the Central Research Institute, a 100-year-old institution.

What he liked the most about Kasauli was its salubrious climate, pine-scented air and long walks in the company of tiny birds – the Himalayan barbets, crows, koel, bulbuls, mynahs, Simla tits. Hillsides bedecked with wild flowers mesmerised him and he felt one with the cosmos as he walked on these roads listening to the melodious chirping of birds.

As Kasauli had once been a British cantonment, many times he met people who came to visit homes they once lived in and to go round its cemeteries including those located in the nearby cantonments of Subathu and Dagshai to locate their ancestors' tombstones. Swami Ramanand watched these people who came from so far-off and wondered about the strange desire of humans to cling to worldly affairs, neglecting their real quest. Why don't they search for their real roots and try to unite with the real Father? He never understood. Another thing that puzzled him was the desire to own a second home in the hills. *Kothis* at Kasauli sold for crores of rupees and it was this mad desire to make money that was causing problems for their ashram. The good man who had donated land to their ashram had died and his children, hand-in-glove with builders and local revenue staff, were plotting to take back the land. How could man be so selfish, he thought and the next moment the thought crossed his mind that the ashram's desire to save the land was also selfish. He had no answer to so many questions ... he needed to meditate more.

The organisation set-up by Swami Ramanand's Guru ji was one of the richest in the area. They had all the modern day comforts in the ashram. They travelled in Esteems and Safaris, and Guru ji had a Mercedes. They were computer friendly and tech savvy. They had a website and corresponded on e-mail with Guru ji's office for all organisational matters.

As Swami Ramanand and his disciple sat in the car he made up his mind, enough was enough. He would tell Guru ji, make it clear to him that he was uncomfortable and wanted *mukti* from his administrative job.

The driver sped towards Solan town and Ramanand saw hawkers selling farm fresh *bhuttas* roasted on charcoal amber, smeared with salt, pepper, and lemon juice, fresh cucumbers and radishes, sugar cane juice, spicy *chaat*. The wheel of life was moving always, he thought.

Soon they had entered the raucous Solan bazaar ... the market was buzzing with people, each shop was crowded. This desire to buy and sell ... is this normal? he asked himself. Is this thing we call civilisation normal ... TVs, telephones, all this technology and mad rush towards materialism coupled with a sharp decline of values? Where was the world going?'

They had reached the DC's office. He realised that they had not checked about the availability of the DC. 'Will the DC meet us? We don't have any prior appointment,' he asked his disciple.

'You do not need a prior appointment Swami ji. Everyone respects Guru ji and meets us without appointment, *sab guruji ki kripa hai*,' (It is all Guruji's grace) aid his disciple confidently.

In a way he was right. He had realised in the last couple of years that even after becoming a Swami you do not shed your ego and the more senior you became in an organisation the more egoistic you became.

Then he heard his disciple say, 'But I never take chances. Before we started from Kasauli, I had telephoned the PA of the DC. She is available in the office today.'

'She?'

'Yes, the DC is a lady. Madam's name is Manisha.'

Swami Ramanand stopped. His heartbeat increased. He felt dizzy. Manisha ... Oh God ... Would the world that

THE SANYASI | 109

he had renounced never leave him? How could it be possible? Was she the same Manisha?

'Swami ji let us go. Why have we stopped?' said his disciple.

'You said, what is her name . . .?' he could not take that name. For years he had kept it buried deep down in his heart – the very heart that was now beating. For him, the heart beats of love had stopped long ago. He felt suffocated. He had difficulty in breathing. The very thought that she could be sitting there just a few feet ahead of him made him tremble.

'Her name is Manisha Katoch. She is from Himachal. She studied at St Bedes College. Her father was a senior officer in the government.' His disciple had done his homework well.

'She is the same,' he whispered as sweat trickled down his temples.

'Are you fine, Swami ji?'

'Yes. No. We have to go back to the ashram,' he said feebly, trying to gather his composure.

The disciple was taken aback. What was wrong with Swami ji? He had never seen him so pale before. And to his horror he saw Swami ji swaying as if he would fall down. Swami ji took his support as the duo returned to the car.

Once the Swami ji said something it had to be obeyed, his disciple knew. There was no room for argument or explanation. When they arrived at Kasauli, Swami Ramanand was still in a state of shock. He was numb with the revelation of who he was going to come face-to-face with. From the demeanour his disciples and other inmates knew that their young Swami ji was under acute stress. They did not disturb or bother him as he entered his *kutia* unaware of what was happening around him.

It was only when he was alone that Swami Ramanand was able to face himself. His hands and legs were still trembling. He sat down to calm himself.

Manisha – she was the reason he took sanyas. Because of her he had left everything – renounced the world including his responsibilities. And the guilt of that decision was still within him.

It was the year 1992, when his parents died. Being the eldest he had taken over the family business. As he had to leave college, he joined the B. Com. course at the Government Evening College on the Mall. It was there that he first saw her. She used to come to the college library. He started visiting the library, just to be near her.

He was not Swami Ramanand then but Shailender. He had fallen head over heels in love with her. She had big black eyes. Her smile was like sunshine and it warmed his heart.

For one full year all he could think of was her. That year came back to him as clearly as if it were yesterday.

She was the most beautiful girl he had ever seen. He started to follow her everywhere – when she strolled on the Mall with her friends, to her home in the Benmore area and when she went for tuitions to Brockhurst.

As if this was not crazy enough he started going to her house in the middle of the night to stand below her window and watch the light burning in her room as she studied. He would walk from Sanjauli to Chota Shimla and then climb up past the Barnes Court to reach Benmore. He would cross the haunted Churail Bauri between St Bedes Chowk and Chota Simla. But he was so engrossed in love that he barely noticed anything eerie about the place. During the day he would think about the rumours that a woman in a red sari would appear out of nowhere and roam there at midnight.

The warmth of his love for her was all he needed. For him the sun shone at night in the shape of that 100W light bulb in her house.

After worshipping at the altar of his beloved's house he would return to Sanjauli. He took a different route every time to avoid the patrolling policemen. At times, he was stopped by the policemen on night duty. He had to make excuses . . . he was going to the hospital, he was returning from a marriage, he had been to his friend's house who met with an accident . . . .

He was blissfully involved in his one-sided love affair when his dream world crumbled around him.

'Oh, God,' Swami Ramanand sighed as he recalled his agony when Shimla celebrated that their girl had cleared the IAS exam.

He knew that now he had lost whatever chance he had. All his dreams and ideas of taking care of her, of tenderness and love, of marriage and family were shattered. He felt lifeless. She left to join the Academy. He lost interest in business and family.

He started to read religious books and listen to devotional songs. The desire to renounce this material world and to immerse himself in the quest for eternal love started to grow stronger. He went to several ashrams and interacted with various *mahatmas*. He held long discussions with his friends about the futility of life. None of his friends knew about his love for Manisha and the reason for his sudden bend towards religion, but they spent hours sitting in roadside *dhabas* and on the forest road to debate the merits and demerits of this world. All this time Shailender was looking for a spiritual teacher.

When he found his Guru ji, he renounced the world which had no attraction for him anymore and became a sanyasi. He told everything to his Guru ji, who listened patiently and did not ask any questions. He gave him *deeksha* and accepted him as a disciple. He also gave him a new name and new identity. From Shailender he became Swami Ramanand.

Swami Ramanand took out his old bag. It was the same bag with which he had come to the ashram fifteen years ago. Several times he had thought of burning whatever it contained, but he could not cut this umbilical cord to his past. He hesitated for a moment but then decided to open it after all these years.

It contained all those gifts that he had bought for her but never had the courage to give. Every month he purchased one card from any of the card shops on the Mall – Batish, Asia

THE SANYASI | 113

Book Depot or Minerva and penned his feelings for her. All those cards were there. There were key-chains, lockets with the letters M and S, books and small teddies, bangles and the letters that he wrote to her but never posted . . . .

Why had he kept this bag with him all these years? He felt drained and empty. He needed to take a decision.

Swami Ramanand did not come out of his room that day. He had no food, no water and by the next morning his decision was made. It was she who was instrumental in making him a sanyasi and now he would go back to the world that he had relinquished for her. He could not face her as a Swami.

Shailender could not escape from love. She had altered the course of his life again without her knowing anything.

1992

14

The Ghost Who Loved

It was the year 1995.

Lighting a cigarette Sanjay looked sideways at his friend Jack. He had come from England specially to visit Shimla. They had met at Oxford University where Sanjay was doing a course in world history and Jack was studying anthropology.

'Isn't life weird? Sometimes you feel that there is a pattern. A minutely detailed design. You were destined to light a cigarette here in Shimla in my company at this moment,' said Jack.

'Sometimes? What about other times?'

'Other times it all appears so very absurd, haphazard and unplanned. An accident,' he said softly.

They sat in a comfortable silence on the bench in front of the Oberoi Clarkes Hotel, watching the sun behind the distant hills. The blue–green mountains rolled in humps one after the other in succession. And the Shimla hill-slope was starting to shimmer with the glow of tiny lights which were being switched on one by one in countless box-like houses and shops.

'You know this Ridge of Shimla creates two separate watersheds. Water flowing down to the eastern side mingles with the Bay of Bengal whereas the one that flows down the western side mixes with the Arabian Sea.'

Jack listened and marvelled at the wonders of nature. He did not say anything.

"What do you think?' Sanjay asked casually after some time.

'Of what?' asked Jack looking at his Indian friend with amusement.

'Of everything, the place, the people, the ambience and so on,' he gestured.

There was silence again. Jack said nothing. Shimla, how he'd wanted to be here! And he was here at last. A dream. He had heard so many adventurous stories of the place from his grandfather that, after his death, he felt the urge to come here. He wanted to see the place with his own eyes. It was here his grandfather had spent the most memorable years of his life.

Jack was overwhelmed. He diverted his attention towards two fat monkeys sitting on the railing on their left, watching the passersby.

'Their actions are so similar to that of humans,' he broke his silence.

'Watch them pounce on people carrying shopping bags especially ladies.'

And truly baring their teeth they charged on their targets. Unfortunately, for them, they did not succeed in snatching a bag, though they scared the life out of a young girl who screamed loudly and ducked behind an elderly couple who had stopped to watch the setting sun.

'Come on, let's go, its getting chilly, the shop will close.' Sanjay said. They walked towards the Mall which bustled with life – the brightly-lit shops and the elegant crowd. Though young school and college going girls and boys clad in fashionable outfits were more visible because of their number, the sophisticated older generation attired in three-piece-suits and silk sarees were the ones that charmed Jack. Both for strolling and shopping the Mall was a happening place.

Jack wanted to go to the Maria Book Store, the antique bookshop on the Mall. His grandfather had been quite friendly with the owner. 'I want to just go there and browse through the books, no need to tell the present owner about my grandpa. I just want to feel the place and smell the past through the books . . .,' he had told Sanjay.

His grandfather, an army man, had served for over five years at Calcutta before being posted to Simla in 1940. He was a security officer at the Viceregal Lodge. His wife wasn't with him. She hadn't wanted to leave her luxurious and civilised life for a place called India. Moreover, she had heard horrifying stories about the natives, their customs, traditions, their poverty and backwardness. Jack's grandparents separated later, and Jack's father, a twelve-year-old boy at that time had stayed with his mother. It was later when Jack's dad got married that his grandparents patched up. It was Jack's mother who helped bridge the divide.

Then Jack's parents died in an accident. He was just four years old then. His grandfather took care of him and became his mother, father and friend.

'What exactly do you remember about Simla or long for when you are away?' Jack asked as he watched a group of young girls clad in blue jeans, high boots with shoulder length hair marching towards them. He pushed his friend gently a little to the left so as to prevent the collision. The girls giggled as they passed them. It was Saturday evening and the Mall was overcrowded.

'That's a difficult question. You can't exactly pin point. I yearn for everything, the ambience, the weather: mist filled valleys of the monsoon months, bright sunny days of April and October, cool showers in summer and snow flakes in winter. I remember when I was a child my mother was irritated by the rain. For days sun wouldn't come out and it would drizzle non-stop for ten days sometimes. The clothes that she washed would not dry and that irritated her further. In winters she would work hard to burn coal fires. We brothers and sisters would huddle under heavy cotton quilts and relate ghost stories,' Sanjay narrated nostalgically.

'Ghost stories? I wonder if some are real. This reminds me of grandpa, he too used to tell me so many stories of

Simla. The love that he felt for this town radiated on his face,' Jack said.

Jack also felt that his grandfather had left a part of himself here. Then one day he'd received a letter from India that changed everything. Jack heard him sobbing. He would sit silently for hours, brooding. A couple of days later he suffered a heart attack.

Eventually, to Jack's relief, he started talking again when he gained a little of his strength. Earlier his stories were of the balls, the parties and the big-wig Britons, Viceregal Lodge, its natural beauty but now he talked more about the hardworking natives, their honesty and sincerity.

There was Raja, the stable boy with whom he had become friendly. Then there was Mr Sud of Maria Books, an educated man who knew everything about Simla and discussed the latest books, gazetteers, maps of the Simla hills, etc. He admired Suraj, the head gardener of Viceregal Lodge, for his love of plants and flowers.

Jack one day teasingly asked his grandfather whether he had ever fallen in love with a native girl. The wrinkled face of the old man lit up suddenly. It radiated love but in his eyes Jack could see intense pain. It was then that he told him about her, his love in Simla.

'We did not have to speak; we knew each other's innermost thoughts and feelings. There was a bond that united us across nations and cultures. It was love, pure and simple,' said his grandfather. 'It is not possible to be in love with a place if you don't love a person there,' he added. He narrated the story of the pretty *Paharan* girl Lata, a milkmaid.

He met her by accident. In fact, she had an accident. She had twisted her ankle and was moaning with pain when he came across her during his morning stroll in Boileauganj. She was very shy and would not look at him directly. Her eyes were fixed elsewhere. Her vulnerability, simplicity and beauty attracted him. After a few weeks their friendship began to grow and despite the language barrier they began spending time in each other's company everyday.

Slowly, she became bolder and began to visit the Shiv Temple below Boileauganj with him. He felt at ease with her. He was so smitten by this exquisite native girl with large big eyes that several times in a day he would endearingly assure her that he would take her along to England.

However, his departure from Simla was sudden. He could not inform her. He received orders to leave for Delhi at 11 pm on 15 July 1947 because of the communal chaos. From Delhi he had to leave for England. He did not get a chance to return to Simla.

Initially he didn't suffer too much guilt. The guilt came when he received a letter many years later informing him of her death. She had died a spinster. All those years she had waited for him, expecting him to take her to England as promised. The letter was written by one Mr Rana Singh, her neighbour. He blamed him for keeping her waiting and heartbroken. He also claimed that her spirit roamed near the Shiv Temple because she did not die in peace.

A few days after Jack's grandfather had related this story, he breathed his last. But before his death, he made Jack promise that he will go to Simla and ask forgiveness on his behalf at Shiv temple.

Years later, as luck would have it, Jack met Sanjay at Oxford who was not only an Indian but was from Simla. They became friends and Sanjay invited him to visit his country and be his guest.

It took another four years for his dream to materialise. This was now his second day in Shimla. Though he had 'seen' the town, roads, schools, trees, and Mall through the 'eyes' of his grandfather, the sensation of actually seeing it was altogether different. The place was so different from what he had imagined, but it had to be different. His grandfather had described a much younger Simla.

'So, what is your mission? You mentioned something,' asked Sanjay.

'Tomorrow I want to go to the Jakhu Temple and meet the monkeys there! And then you have to take me to the Shiv Temple near Boileauganj the day after, that is Monday morning.'

'You really know a lot about Simla.'

'I want to go there early in the morning, the Shiv temple. There is a temple there, isn't it?' he said, dreading that it was no more there after so many years.

'There was a temple some fifteen years back, when I had gone there with my mom on an Indian festival Shivratri. I've never been there since,' Sanjay said.

'It's the one covered with thick Deodar and Oak trees and you have to cross a railway line. I hope, it's still there,' Jack said.

'Well, as you know the place so very well, it won't be very tough finding it. It will be there because once an Indian temple is built somewhere it stays forever. But first we have to go to the Hanuman temple at Jakhu.'

Jack was amused to see the clever monkeys at Jakhu temple. They came near him without any fear. A tiny one climbed on his shoulder and searched his shirt pocket. Two others grabbed one leg each and searched his trouser pockets. While the three searched him thoroughly many others looked with anticipation.

Thanks to the advice given by Sanjay he had nothing in his pockets, no glasses, no wallet. The way these monkeys searched his pockets they could be employed at airports to frisk passengers, Jack mused. When they did not find anything they left him in disgust and walked away.

After a while the friends walked down to the Richmond area. It was cold here. Sanjay told him that the British used to have ice-wells here. These were huge pits that accumulated winter snow. It lasted through the summer months and came handy in chilling beer.

After that, they walked past the United Services (US) Club with its maroon roof buildings. Sanjay informed Jack that it was here that the Radcliff Boundary Commission drew the lines that portioned India and Pakistan.

Jack felt as if he were breathing history.

The next day, the friends started early. The sun had not yet risen. It took them more than an hour to reach the temple from Tutikandi. From Boileauganj they took the bifurcation to Summer Hill and after five minutes took another bifurcation. On the way they crossed several houses and colonies. The temple was a mere 200 metres ahead of these concrete structures but was still amidst a thick grove of trees.

'It's quite big. Grandpa said it was a very small temple,' whispered Jack.

'What's the matter? You are staring at the temple with such obeisance as if it is your God, aren't you a Christian?' asked Sanjay awkwardly. He was becoming irritated by the demands of his foreigner friend, including getting up so early to visit temples!

'Yes, for now this is my God, where should I leave my shoes?'

'Anywhere here,' said Sanjay pointing to the space ahead of them below the stairs leading to the temple.

Both of them washed their hands at the *bauri* (water well) below the road. Jack was puzzled to see that the water was flowing continuously and there was no tap to close it. It was water from a perennial natural spring, Sanjay informed him, seeing his bewilderment.

There was something peculiar about them, a casual Indian and a devout white man. Jack's face portrayed anxiety, determination and reverence.

Jack took deep breaths to calm his nerves, he was standing at the same place where his grandfather had stood five decades back. While his grandfather came with a frail and beautiful girl, he was here to ask for forgiveness for the wrong done to her. He didn't know how to ask for mercy from this Indian God. 'Please, forgive him, I have come for him, let both of them rest in peace,' he murmured. For a few seconds he stood quietly, then opened his eyes. Awkwardly he bent his head in front of the stone deity to pay obeisance.

He didn't even know whether the Indian God had heard him. Disheartened he stared around. Had he come so far just to stand there and say 'sorry'? He could have done that anywhere, he thought dejectedly.

'Come and take *prashad* from the Panditji,' called Sanjay. Jack turned towards the priest, he thrust forward his right palm, drank the drops of cool water poured through a small kettle, ran his palm on the top of his head, extended his hand again for the white sugary tablets. Then an idea struck him.

'Sanjay, ask him how you get to know that your prayers have been answered?' Sanjay shrugged, talked to the Pandit in Hindi. To Jack's surprise, the priest gave a flower to him, pointing towards the stone idol.

'He says go and place the flower on top of the lingam. If it falls down, whatever you have asked for will be granted. However, there is no time limit. Sometimes it takes days to fall down,' said his friend with a smug smile.

Jack respectfully placed the flower on top of the idol and closed his eyes praying for forgiveness.

'Hey, the flower has fallen down!' he heard his friend's surprised voice. He opened his eyes to see the flower at the base of the stone idol. He was dumb-struck for a few moments.

'My prayers have been answered, I have been forgiven. Grandpa has been forgiven,' he joyously shouted.

'Hey, stop shouting,' Sanjay laughed.

'One more thing please, ask the priest whether a spirit or ghost or whatever you call it, that of a *Paharan* girl is seen here?'

'Don't be stupid, let's go.'

"Please, for me, just one question, it's important.'

Sanjay looked at his friend's pleading face, hesitated and then turned to the Pandit. Jack waited anxiously. He wasn't surprised with the reply.

'He says a few people have come across a woman here. She has been spotted in the night sometimes sitting near the water bauri and sometimes walking along the stretch between the temple and the railway line. Some have heard her weeping and wailing. He himself has never seen her. That was a very strange question, did your grandpa also tell you about an Indian Ghost?' Sanjay asked in a lighter tone.

Jack gave a knowing smile. Not caring if anyone understood him or not, he said 'Her spirit will not come again. She is in peace now. Grandpa has been forgiven.'

1995

15

Love@www

'Ours was a whirlwind romance. But with a difference. It was on the Internet. I am tech savvy and in 2004 Reliance launched CDM phones on which you could surf the net. I was one of the first in the town to have it. It was a new feature at that time. You could check your e-mails but only on rediffmail. So I opened a rediff account. In mid-September while checking my mail there was a flash advertisement and I saw her photograph, I fell in love,' said Homi.

'I had never noticed these advertisements earlier. But there was something in her face that hooked me.'

'Well I can't say if it was love at first sight from my side,' said Rimi reminiscing that phase five years ago, 'I was a software professional working on the web edition of a leading newspaper in Shillong. You see, I had to be on the net every time and for me it was just "fun" putting my ad on the rediff matchmaking site. I wasn't serious about it.

Now when I think about it, maybe I was a little worried at that time because my parents were looking for a match and belonging to a conservative family I was a little apprehensive of what kind of an "arranged marriage" I will land into. So I thought lets' see what happens.'

Her's was for fun, his was purpose.

'When I saw her face in that ad', Homi says, 'I had to locate her. She was mine and mine only. I was unregistered on the rediff matchmaking site. The first thing that I did was got registered, paid about rupees 700 to get in contact with her. I belong to an open-minded, liberal family. My sister while loading my profile didn't include our surname, Chatterjee, because we thought it would restrict marriage options. Only Bengalis will come forward (I wish I knew!) I sent this profile to her on e-mail – "I saw your profile. Please check mine." I also sent her my best photograph, it was a shot taken of me at Chalet Naldehra.'

'Well, I had got more than 500 replies for that ad,' said Rimi as she listened affectionately to her two-year-old daughter's jumble-bumble. 'His was also one of them. I just saw his name Homi Kumar and thought that he is some Bihari or UP guy. Moreover, his photograph never impressed me. Actually, I am not into looks. And I must tell you that even during our Internet courtship he sent me four to five photographs and in everyone he looked different. So I never focused on his photos. I replied back by e-mail, "Sorry, we are looking for a Brahmin Bengali alliance".'

'See, we were destined to meet,' says Homi laughing, 'I too am a Brahmin and a Bengali so I shot another e-mail, this time a two-page-long – all about myself and my family.'

'Yes, he is right, it was this e-mail of his, long and detailed which aroused my interest. Though still up till now my *funda* of "let me see what happens" hadn't changed; I was not serious but started corresponding on the e-mail.'

'We exchanged more than 150 mails,' chuckled Homi.

'Then he contacted me on the phone, and I was surprised how he got my number,' said Rimi.

'Well, thanks to the Internet,' said a beaming Homi, 'it was so easy to get her number. I knew that she worked for this paper in Shillong. So I got the number from their website.'

'Really, it was such a shock for me to hear his voice at 5.30 in the morning. My work timings were scheduled from 5.30 to 8.30 every morning, I had to upload the latest news on the website of the paper. But I liked his voice. Then I told my mom just like that, very casually, nothing serious. I am very friendly and close with my mom. Everyday she used to ask me how many proposals I got in response to my marriage ad. She was quite amused with the whole idea though wondered how two people can agree to marriage on computer.'

'She gave me her residence number,' said Homi.

'He called the very next day and I was very surprised. My mom picked up the phone and he said that "he was

Homi Chatterjee calling from Simla and wanted to speak to Rimi".'

'Well, I decided long ago that this is the girl for me. So I had called to announce the marriage date. It was to be 25 November.'

'Yes, this was really crazy. I told him that he was going bonkers, we did not even know each other. And what about my family; my father will have a heart attack if he hears this bull shit,' I informed him.

'I didn't care. I told her that I was coming to her place to meet her parents,' he said.

'Now I was a little scared. Dad had to be told. It was my mom, she did a wonderful job. She first casually told him about the *rishta-fishta* on the net and how the world was changing. Dad, all my relatives including cousins were dead against the idea. They just could not comprehend as how an alliance can be made through the web. But hats off to my mom for all her support.'

'Yes, it was she who convinced her dad to see the boy.'

'So with grumbling father who had total mistrust about this relationship and an anxious mother, I went to the Airport to receive him on 23 December.'

'I had landed three hours ago and they were not there,' Said Homi, 'The next thing was I sent an SMS to her.'

'It was a traffic jam, we got stuck in it, you know those long army convoys of the north-east, they take lot of time and no one gives a pass. I was so worried on what he will think about us. He had come from so far and here we were so late.'

'I was adamant that they should come to pick me up so I waited.'

'You know what, when I saw him I felt as if I had known him forever.'

'Even earlier when we talked on phone and e-mailed, it was as if we knew each other since ages. We were comfortable,' he adds.

'So at Airport, it was 'hi' and 'hi' and I introduced my parents to him.'

'Oh, we forgot to mention the biggest constraint in our so-called courtship.'

'I reside in Shillong, Meghalaya on the other end of the country, away from this beautiful State. It was natural that even after my parents met him they had reservations.'

'They did not want to send their daughter so far off.'

'This time I put my foot down, it had to be Homi.'

'Her parents had to go to Jaipur for an official convention. On way back they came to Shimla to confirm whether we exist,' laughed Homi.

'Ya, that is right. Then both our parents met at Delhi,' said Rimi. 'Now our marriage was officially clear. What a relief!' she added.

'And then I got her e-mail openly exhibiting love. What a day it was!'

Her mail:

From: Sulekha Chakraborty on Fri, 21 Jan '05 @ 08:09 AM

I dream of a dream today, a dream of an evening, when sitting side by side, holding each others' hands, feeling the soothing breeze of the waves, 'together' we dream of a better tomorrow. Yes dear, there are thousands of dreams in my heart, with every dream I live, for every dream I die. To have you in my life as a part of reality is a dream indeed, but more so, you are central to my beautiful dreams of life. Now that, I feel ur presence even when u r not around; I feel the warmth of ur touch, even when you stand apart. I hear the beautiful song of life, even when u keep astounding quiet; I know that my soul is touched by ur love even when u say nothing at all.

If in every moment, I feel that I am being studied by ur eyes, if every day I endeavour to look beautiful when u pass by; and if in every moment of my grief and suffering I feel the strength of ur support, then how do I term my feelings for u ... I know not what it is... if this is what being in love is, then yes I'am in love ... in love with u. No my dear, there is no difference between life & death; if one is in 'LOVE', for I only live for that person who takes my breath away ... Just a glance of urs infuses Life into myself and leaves me STONE-DEAD, too. I can now remember the beautiful lines of Mirza Galib once who wrote ...,

'Mohabbat mein nahin hain fark jine aur marne ka'
Usi ko dekh kar jite hain, jis kafer pe dam nikle'

Hoping that the feelings of my heart taking the shelter of these words touches ur heart, that through love as the only language of love, I can convey to u, what u mean to me. U give me enough reasons to dream ... I dream for that evening, when living 'LIFE TOGETHER', we can dream of a NEW DAY, a NEW LOVELY LIFE.

Even if the world ends tonight, I would still die as one who has known the 'magic' of being in love, one who has risen in love and has allowed love to rise more & more in the heart ... thats' of course, only because of u ... but I want to live my life with u in ur love till my last breath.

Its Urs, only urs ... Rimi.

'The support and love that I got through his mails was my lifeline during our courtship,' said Rimi seriously.

His mail:

HOMI KUMAR *wrote: 25TH JAN 2005 18:47:42*

MY DEAR RIMI
RIMI, today I want a commitment that you will be always beside me till my last...

We will work together for the best things life have to offer, but at the same time always be prepared for the worst .... but will be together all the time ... living as a one unit. A unit welded with love, supported with understanding and coated with passion.

Rimi, I want you to live life not just spend it ... find some passion ... validate your existence on this earth, it is not that you have to study or have to do something in academics, but try to create something new, enjoy life ... FIND YOUR PASSION AND EXCEL IN IT ... 10% of the people create and live, 90% watch and spend ... I want you to always in the first category ... I will not appreciate your saying that I am doing nothing ... Life means action ... if you are doing nothing, you have shorten your life ... try to create events, as we measure our life by events and not by time ...

Excuse me if I am sounding like preacher...

Missing you my love ... Let's make life more fulfilling ... together.

RIMI'S HOMI

'Then the next hurdle was the timing of our marriage.'

'My father was not in for an early marriage,' clarified Rimi.

'My father, Sanat Kumar Chatterjee, called her dad and told him that if he doesn't agree for an early marriage, it may not take place at all. He being an astrologer informed her father that his stars indicated that the boy will change his mind soon and become a *sadhu*.'

'He said to my father, "think of me as girl's father and not as boy's, take my advice and fix an early date",' said Rimi affectionately.

'So on 2 March 2005 we got married at Shillong. My *baraat* had six people.'

'A day before our marriage his parents, brother and sister saw me for the first time,' recalls Rimi with fondness.

'I believe in destiny,' said Homi, 'our birthdays fall on the same day, though different months. We were born on the same day – Saturday. None of us drinks tea. And there are so many other similar things.'

'It is like what he thinks I think and many times we say the same thing at the same time. For us Internet is the greatest matchmaker and we are thankful for it.' Rimi said with love in her eyes.

2004-2005

16

My Parents' Love Story

I am Akshita, I was born in 1993 in Shimla at Lady Reading Hospital. This tale is my parents' love story – inseparable by death and loss. I do not know whether all children think that their parents' love story is unique, but I feel it is so.

Till five years ago, when I was nearing twelve, it never occurred to me that my parents too had a beautiful love story. Maybe, at such a tender age I did not know what love is. Our family was like any other middle-class family, busy in the hum-drum of day-to-day existence.

My father is a journalist and my mother a school teacher. I have a younger brother Anubhav, who was nine years old then.

My father used to get up early and make a cup of tea for mom every morning before she began her busy day. She used to cherish that moment sipping it slowly giving loving looks to all three of us. This was a high point and the treasured moment in her life. This was their love which I never realised then. In fact, I never took notice of it, the child that I was, but now I realise how precious it was.

My parents' marriage had no melodrama; it was an arranged marriage. Both of them belonged to Jammu. It was *Shivratri* that day when my father, accompanied by a family friend, met my mom's brother to talk about the marriage proposal. The three of them headed for mamu's house totally unscheduled and unplanned. She served tea to them, unaware of the marriage prospects. She thought he was her brother's client. That was all. For him, it was love at first sight, no romantic illusions, no personal interviews and no words exchanged. My father's search for the soulmate ended right there.

I wonder how they could have agreed to spend all their lives with each other without knowing anything – likes, dislikes, hobbies, desires and then of course, love, I mean they did not love each other at that time, they had just seen each other, not even talked.

They were married and my mother came to Shimla. I cannot say much about their time then, and a year later I was born. As there was no one from the family my father was the first person who held me when the nurse brought me out of the labour room – all pink, wrinkled and howling.

Three years later my brother was born. We had stayed eleven years in Shimla when my father was posted to Raipur, Chhattisgarh – the newly created Indian State. I remember he was so disturbed to be sent so far off. It was my mother who took it in her stride and brought him out of despair.

I recall her organising and packing everything in the house efficiently. I was a child but I was so impressed by her positive attitude. She was our backbone and it was because of her that I now realise we had settled so well in a new place.

And then on 13 May 2005, she was no more. Her very existence was wiped away from this earth. It was as if she was never alive. She died suddenly of a cardiac arrest, a term I heard for the first time. She was only thirty-nine years old. We were with her when she collapsed in the early morning. Minutes before, she was in intense conversation with us about the day's shopping plans. But, unexpectedly it was all over and the world had come crashing down on us.

We had come for our holidays to Jammu and were at mamu's place. Father was at Raipur. I remember telling my nine-year-old brother, 'Everything is fine, they have taken mother to the hospital. Father is coming today.'

At 3 o'clock in the night my father arrived. I saw him crying for the first time. He was howling inconsolably. I felt as if someone had crushed my heart with cold hands.

My father asked everyone, 'Did she say anything . . . did she leave any message . . . she must have said something before she left.' I could not comprehend what he meant at that time but now I realise he just wanted a token, a memento of love, something to look forward to, something tangible while she took her last breath, something for him to live on. He could not even clasp her to him in her last moments. His other statement is entrenched in my mind, 'I don't even know where the children's socks are, what will I do without her, my kids will never get her touch, or feel?' At that tender age I was surprised that my father was worried about our socks when so much had happened and our lives had shattered. Of course, it was not our socks, it was his life which he had lost.

Shakespeare in one of his sonnets wrote: 'Loves' not times' fool . . . love alters not with his grief, hours and weeks.' He might have written this for my parents because their love story, so short in years, is timeless and is embedded in faith and hope. It began in the year 1992.

To mom, Shimla was her home. She fell in love with this hill town on the first day that she arrived here. She did not loose any opportunity and moment to be with nature and was curious and raring to explore the place. She was passionate about watching films in the cinema hall. We visited different locations in the surroundings – Mashobra, Kufri, Cregneno whenever a film unit came with stars including Govinda, Manisha Koirala, Bobby Deol, Raveena Tandon and many more and she was thrilled like a child.

For her, Shimla weather was the icing on the cake. Every season had its own beauty for her. Winters were all white, snow enveloped the hills and valleys. These cold winter months passed slowly and warmed to comfortable summers.

Whenever day temperature rose a little above normal quick showers would cool down the town. Long monsoon months would bring mist, fog and the romance of getting wet in the downpour. Layers of mist would settle everywhere ... in the hills, valleys and the mighty trees looked waiflike wrapped in thick blanket of fog. From our house in US Club she could see the evening colours of different hues spread on the horizon. At times, it used to rain cats and dogs for an hour or so and then bright sun would come out with the rainbow so clear. Then the autumn, when Oak trees shed their leaves and she walked on that silver carpet crunching them underneath her feet, the sound startlingly loud because of the quietness all around. The evergreen *Deodars* and other pine trees remained green even in autumn. She loved every day, every season here in Shimla ...

The occasion that brought her most joy and excitement was the *Karva Chauth* on the Ridge. She used to eagerly wait for the festival days before and on the day of the festival all decked up we used to reach the Ridge carrying the *thali* and the sweets. My father used to bring *Gujhia* from a sweet shop in Sanjauli and *samosas* from Vijay Sweets in Middle Bazaar, these were her two favourite eating joints. The closest friends that she made in her life were Shimalites and she cherished their friendship forever.

Her dream was to settle down in Shimla and own a small duplex cottage aesthetically designed with local architecture. Another desire left unfulfilled was that she could not travel on the narrow gauge Kalka–Shimla rail. It fascinated her. But alas, her dreams just remained dreams.

Their love could not have been more true or more lasting. But who can blame destiny.

My father cursed himself for not being with her that day. He could not even see her once, just one last time. How many times he must have thought that he could have died with her. Till then, he did not know that there could be such a sorrow.

Life had taken a turn, a miserable turn for us. However, gradually in the last five years I have seen it changing. It is mom's love that keeps him going. All that love I had not seen earlier, I see now.

On request, he was posted again at Shimla – where he started fifteen years back. We came to the same house. Some well-wishers told him that it was not the right decision but he stuck to it. Loving photographs of mom – alone, with us, with papa – were hung in all the rooms. The furniture was adjusted as she had adjusted it earlier and so was the kitchen, books and curtains. He used to sit quiet for hours looking at walls – perhaps, to get strength and courage to move ahead.

For two years it was a very trying time for all of us, but more so for my father. He took care of two children aged 9 and 12 singlehandedly. He brought cards on mom's birthday, their marriage anniversary and got her favourite dishes prepared on these occasions. He also went to the temple and started keeping fast which he never did earlier. 'Nisha is with me here, why should I worry?' became his high point.

He doted on us, exactly the way mama used to do. He took care of all our needs. He said all the strength came to him because of mom's love.

He prayed to God which he had never done earlier and asked mom, wherever she had gone, to give him strength to take care of us and help him to make the children grow up into good human beings that she always wanted them to be. He cared for us in sickness and health. At times, I have seen him sobbing his heart out in loneliness and despair. Nobody knows the anguish and misery that pervaded our house during that time.

There were times when he was ill but could not afford to be ill. He realised that we needed him and he felt that God and Mama answered his prayers for strength. One night when he was dreadfully exhausted and angry at his fate, he was sobbing when he realised that my brother slipped in the bathroom and hurt his head. He forgot all his worries and ran to the doctor. I look back and remember all the ailments, the falls, the tantrums that we had and how stressed and muddled he must have been. He used to hurry home from his office just to attend to us. How removed he was from the carefree husband he used to be when mom was alive.

But he carried on and to this day he is carrying on. Every Sunday and on holidays he takes us out to visit different places and on other days comes back home early in the evening to have dinner with us. I am going to be seventeen now and my brother fourteen. My mom is not here but we are happy and count our blessings to have such a father. His face glows with pride when someone remarks, how intelligent and good mannered Nisha's children are.

This has been possible because my parents loved each other so much. My father's unfailing love and devotion to his wife for the last five years has made us grow into responsible individuals. And if one could turn the clock backwards I do not think he would have exchanged his wife for anyone else, even if they were together just for fourteen years.

He had never imagined that he will have to carry on alone. It must have been such great effort for him to have kept his children so long from realising how desperately sad and lonely he was.

However, I realise my parents' love story has not ended. He may have buried a part of his life, part of himself with her but with us he can laugh and play. For God and mom have given him strength, faith, courage to carry on. He has us to love and be loved and also many happy memories to help him along the road that all must tread. Who knows what future holds.

'You know I want to tell you a secret, when your mom was alive I did not know I loved her so much, it was only when she left me that I realised my intense feelings for her.' He is right, it is because of mom and dad's love that we are what we are and how proud I am to be their daughter. He says that we are the most precious gifts that mom gave him, 'Perhaps, she came into my life to hand over you two and see how much I can do after she leaves the world . . . may be, God had another noble task for her . . . .'

I wonder at what he says and hope it is right.

2010

Glossary

Askalis	Pan Cakes made with white flour/ powdered rice
Bahu	Daughter-in-Law
Bail	Buffalo
Baraat	Marriage Procession
Bauri	Natural Water Point
Besan barfi	Sweet made of gram flour
Beta	Son
Bhabi	Sister-in-Law
Bhuttas	Corn Cobs
Chaat	Spicy savory mix
Chadru	Shawl
Chandhar	Attic
Chullah	Cooking hearth
Churail	Witch
Churidar kurta	Ladies dress – shirt and tight leggings
Deeksha	Initiation ceremony in religious order/sect
Devta	Local God
Dhabas	Small eating joints
Dhar	Ridge

Dhara-re-geet	Popular radio programme of folk songs on AIR Shimla
Dhatu	Headscarf
Dogri(s)	Summer house usually built in pastures
Doodh-Jalebi	Jalebi is an Indian sweet, soaked in sugar syrup which is also had with milk
Dories	Colourful threads tied generally in temples
Dulha	Bridegroom
Dupatta	Indian Scarf/Stole
Fukra	Young man who shows off
Funda	Slang for Fundamental
Ghaas phoos	Insignificant things (phrase)
Golgappa	Sweet n' sour spicy savory
Gujhia	Sweet stuffed with coconut and sugar
Gur	Medium of local devta (god)
Hukkah	Traditional smoking pipe
Kalal	A Caste
Kameez	Shirt
Karva Chauth	Indian festival when women keep fast for their husband's long life
Kothis	Mansions
Koti	Sweater
Kutia	Modest hut (usually of a saint)
Lathi	Stick
Mahatmas	Saints
Maika	Parent's House
Mami	Maternal aunt
Martbaans	Earthen Jar in which pickles are kept
Mash ki daal	Pulse
Mela	Fair
Memsahibs	Ladies

GLOSSARY | 145

Mohalla	Neighbourhood
Mojris	Embroidered leather sandals
Nanad	Husband's sister
Paharan	Hill Woman
Pahari natis	Local hill folk dance
Pahari	Hill folks
Pakki	Permanent
Pankhas	Fan
Patande	Pan Cakes made of wheat flour
Pheras	Ritual during marriage after which ceremony is complete
Potli	Cloth Bag (unstitched)
Prashad	Sweet given to devotees at temples
Rajai	Quilt
Rajmah Chawal	Kidney beans and Rice
Reet	Local Custom
Rishta	Relation (marriage alliance)
Rishta-fishta	Relation (marriage alliance) *slang*
Saas	Mother-in-Law
Sadhu	Saint
Sahibs	Gentlemen
Samosas	Deep fried snack stuffed generally with potatoes
Sasural	House of in-laws
Sati	Custom where widows died at the pyre of their husbands
Sattu	Cakes made with honey, ghee and cereals
Sevaks	Servants (of the local King)
Shehnai	Trumpet, a musical instrument
Siddus	Steamed balls stuffed with poppy seeds made with fermented wheat dough

Sukhi roti	Dry-roti
Suthnu	Tight pyjamas
Thali	Plate
Thoda	Popular ancient folk game of Shimla hills played with bows and arrows
Zenana	Ladies section

References

Chapter 2: The Surprise

The British ladies coming to India in eighteenth century faced many problems. Emily Metcalfe was sent from India to England when she was six, returned at marriageable age and fell in love with Clive Bayley and spent several years in Shimla hills. That the couple did not get to know about Emily's pregnancy is amusing. But the fact that the doctor too did not find out and told her to return to England due to serious illness is hilarious and bizarre at the same time. The life and times of the English ladies in eighteenth and nineteenth century have been chronicled in several books. For reference:

1. Kaye, M.M., *The Golden Calm: An English Lady's Life in Moghul Delhi: Reminiscences by Emily, Lady Clive Bayley and by her father Sir Thomas Metcalfe*, England: Webb & Bower, 1980.
2. Kipling, Rudyard, *Complete Works of Rudyard Kipling*, Hienmann/Octopus, 1978.
3. Nevile, Pran, *Love Stories From the Raj*, Penguin Books, 1995.

Chapter 3: When Rani Became A Boy

Diwan Jarmani Dass, Javier Moro, Ann Morrow and many other writers have recorded the events of the life of Rani Kanari, a simple but intelligent girl from Kangra valley whom Raja Jagatjit Singh of Kapurthala chose as his wife. And this was not a marriage just for the sake of alliance, it was a marriage for love. Following books contain references/details about the life of Rani Kanari and Jagatjit Singh.
1. Dass, Diwan Jarmani, *Maharani*, Hind Pocket Books Limited.
2. Moro, Javier, *Passion India*, Full Circle Books.
3. Morrow, Ann, *The Maharajas of India*, Shrishti Publishers and Distributors.

Chapter 4: Scandal Point

This incident concerning banishment of three Indian princes by Lord Curzon has been recorded by several writers. The main scandal behind the Scandal Point was that the Lady Curzon was photographed in a Sari wearing jewels of Maharaja Patiala Rajinder Singh. Following books contain references to the events and incidents depicted in the story.
1. Dass, Diwan Jarmani, Rakesh Bhan Dass, *Maharani: A fabulous Collection of Adventures of Indian Princesses and Royal Mistresses*, New Delhi: Hind Pocket Books, 2007.
2. Dass, Diwan Jarmani, *Maharaja: Lives and Loves and Intrigues of Indian Princes*, Allied Publishers, 1969.
3. Nadelhoffer, Hans, *Cartier*, Chronicle Books LLC, USA and Thames and Hudson Limited, UK.

4. Morrow, Ann, *The Maharajas of India*, Srishti Publishers and Distributors, 1998.
5. Moro, Javier, *Passion India*, Full Circle Books, 2006.

Chapter 5: The Princess

Brinda, Maharani of Kapurthala has told her tale in her Memoirs which is a moving account of her life. She was born at Jubbal, a princely state in Shimla Hills and at the age of six, she made a promise to herself at Shimla that she would see the world. She did see the world but her life was not smooth. It was full of ups and downs. She died at Shimla.

1. Williams, Elaine, *Maharani: Memoirs of a Rebellious Princess Brinda, Maharani of Kapurthala*, Rupa and Co., 2003.

Chapter 6: Amrita Sher-Gil

Personality of Amrita Sher-Gil was such that she has left so many stories behind that it is difficult to bind these into a single narrative in about two thousand words. That she was a great artist is just one part of her enigmatic personality. Vivan Sundaram, Iqbal Singh, Malcolm Muggeridge and Yashodhara Dalmia have written about her in detail besides so many others. Several individuals have narrated their personal encounters with Amrita and also the stories they heard about her. Baddrudin Tayabji; Khushwant Singh; Karl Khandalavala; Charles Fabri and many others can be named. There is no doubt that Amrita Sher-Gil had a very colourful life. There are several accounts about Amrita's life:

1. Dalmia, Yashodhara, *Amrita Sher-Gil*, Penguin Viking.

2. Hunter, Ian, *Malcolm Muggeridge: A Life*, London: Collins.
3. Khushwant Singh has written about Amrita Sher Gil in his Autobiography and also in numerous other articles.
4. Khandalavala, Karl, *Amrita Sher-Gil*.
5. *Like it Was: The Diaries of Malcolm Muggeridge*, London: Collins, London, 1981.
6. Sundram, Vivan, *Amrita Sher-Gil* (Amrita Sher-Gil by Sundaram, Kapur, Sheikh, Subramanyan)
7. Singh, Iqbal, *Amrita Sher-Gil*
8. Tayabji, Badruddin, *Memoirs of an Egoist*, Roli Books, 1988.

Chapter 7: A Spiritual Bond: Edwina And Jawahar Lal Nehru

The tale of Nehru and Edwina's romance and love has been told by many. All the biographers of Jawahar Lal Nehru, Edwina Mountbatten, Lord Mountbatten and the chroniclers of that era have documented their special relationship. Daughters of Mountbattens and Indira Gandhi, daughter of Jawahar Lal Nehru are on record in admitting that both Edwina and Jawahar Lal Nehru shared a special relationship. Following writers have written about the special bond shared by J. L. Nehru and Edwina.

1. Adams, Jad, Phillip Whitehead, *The Dynasty: The Nehru-Gandhi Story*, Penguin Books and BBC Books, London, 1997.
2. Azad, Maulana Abul Kalam, *India Wins Freedom*, Calcutta: Orient Longmans, 1959.
3. Hough, Richard, *Edwina, Countess Mountbatten of Burma*, London: Weidenfeld & Nicolson, 1983.

4. Hough, Richard, *Mountbatten: Hero of Our Time*, London: Weidenfield and Nicolson, 1980.
5. Moro, Javier, *Passion India*, Full Circle Publishing, 2006.
6. Morgan, Janet, *Edwina Mountbatten: A Life of Her Own*, London: Harper-Collins, 1991.
7. Tunzelmann, Alex Von, *Indian Summer: The Secret History of the End of an Empire*, Simon & Schuster UK Ltd, 2007.
8. *Two Alone, Two Together: Letters Between Jawaharlal Nehru and Indira Gandhi*, Penguin Books India, 2004.
9. Zeiegler, Philip, *Mountbatten, the Official Biography*, London: Collins, 1985.

Chapter 9: Love In Simla

Shimla is one of the favoured locations for film shooting. Love in Simla was shot here and the leading lady Sadhana fell in love with R.K. Nayyar, the director of the movie here in Simla. There are several references to their romance in Simla in books chronicling the history of Bollywood and on the internet. Sadhana has herself spoken about it in her interviews to film magazines.

1. Interview of Sadhana published in *Cine Blitz*, February 1993.
2. Interview of Sadhana published in *Filmfare*, 1991.
3. Telephonic interview with Joy Mukherjee by Shashikant Sharma, Principal Correspondent of *The Tribune* at Shimla.